REMEMBER YOU THIS WAY

THE SOUND OF US BOOK 2

C.R. JANE

Remember You This Way by C. R. Jane

For all the girls who dared to be happy.

THE SOUND OF US SERIES

Remember Us This Way
Remember You This Way
Remember Me This Way

JOIN C.R. JANE'S READERS' GROUP

Stay up to date with C.R. Jane by joining her Facebook readers' group, C.R.'s Fated Realm. Ask questions, get first looks at new books/series, and have fun with other book lovers!

https://www.facebook.com/groups/C.R.FatedRealm

REMEMBER YOU THIS WAY SOUNDTRACK

"Always Remember Us This Way"-
Lady Gaga

"Wilder Minds-
Mumford & Sons

"Wonderland"-
Taylor Swift

"Hate Me"-
Blue October

"Lips of An Angel"-
Hinder

"Born to Love You"-
LANCO

"7 Rings"-
Ariana Grande

"Complicated"-
Olivia O'Brien

"Crash Into Me"-
Dave Matthews Band

"Hope Is A Dangerous Thing For A Woman Like Me To
Have"-
Lana Del Ray

Remember You This Way

Can you ever really start over? It's the question that follows Ariana now that she's reunited with the boys from the Sounds of Us. Haunted by the past and her hopefully soon to be ex-husband, Ari is dragged along as the band continues its world tour.

Touring the world together...it's what they all used to dream about. Sold out stadiums and screaming fans, it's everything anyone would want. But with broken hearts to mend, groupies to ignore, and someone who clearly wants Ariana to leave for good, is their dream more of a nightmare?

Can Ariana find her place in the band before it's too late or is she destined to lose her heart and herself in the process?

She couldn't care less, and I never cared more
So there's no more to say about that
Except hope is a dangerous thing for a woman like me to have
Hope is a dangerous thing for a woman with my past

-Lana Del Rey, Hope Is A Dangerous Thing For A Woman Like Me To Have

PROLOGUE

From the start, the Sounds of Us framed themselves as the quintessential bad boys who had their heart broken and now wouldn't let themselves get close to any other woman. As Jensen said it so bitterly one night on a talk show, "the only thing guaranteed about a woman was that she would break your heart." Flocks of women made it their mission to heal the broken heroes' hearts. They threw themselves at the three band members, offering up everything they possessed for the chance to have one night to change their mind about love. They ate up the band's songs that spoke of a love they longed for but would never have. Only I knew the truth. Once upon a time they did have that love. And I ruined it.

ARIANA

"**D**id she tell you she was married before you fucked her?" says Jensen, the ugly words rolling off his tongue and sending a shiver of dread down my spine. I could feel Jesse tensing in front of me. There was a silent pause in the room as we all absorbed the enormity of what he had just said.

"Jensen, I suggest you get the hell out of my house if you're going to come in here saying shit like that. You're a fucking idiot," snaps Jesse.

My heart sinks at his belief in me. The truth of Jensen's words however is far uglier than he even knows.

Jensen leans against the doorway, a smug expression on his face. He's looking right at me and I know that there must be confirmation that he's telling the truth all over my face with the triumph that flashes in his eyes. Tanner is staring at me too. Disbelief spreads across his face briefly before his entire expression shutters closed. He was always the best out of the three in hiding what he was feeling or thinking. His face is like a blank mask.

Jesse gets off the bed, not bothering to hide the fact that

he's completely naked. Despite the tension in the room I find myself admiring his perfectly sculpted ass, before reminding myself of the seriousness of the situation. Jesse tries to go for nonchalant as he pulls on a pair of sweats that were on the floor, but I can see the rage that he's trying to control in his stiff movements.

"Do I need to walk you out myself?" spits out Jesse, and I cringe at the ugly way he's talking to his best friends.

"Jesse," I say softly. He looks back at me, his face softening.

"It's okay baby. I'll take care of it," he says.

"No, Jesse. This was what I needed to talk to you about."

He turns around slowly, his eyes widening in disbelief. "What you needed to talk to me about? Are you saying it's true...you're fucking married?" he says in a voice laced with pain and disbelief.

"It's more complicated than that," I gasp out, wringing my hands as the situation spins out of control.

"Did you get bored with your husband and just decided that you wanted to fuck a rockstar?" spits out Jensen. "Thought we would be easy prey considering how much you had us wound tight around your finger in high school?"

The three of them look at me with so much loathing that I can barely breathe. In my panic I'm having trouble knowing what to say, remembering what the truth of the matter is...what happened with Gentry just last night.

"My marriage is over," I tell them pleadingly.

"Oh, that's convenient," spits out Jesse. "Did you just think that you would upgrade once you got your claws in us again?" In his rage he tears a picture off the wall and throws it across the room, shattering the glass everywhere.

I start to shake, similar scenes with Gentry darting through my mind and starting a panic attack that I have trouble keeping at bay. As the walls start to close in on me, the sheet I had been holding slips out of my hands, revealing the top half of my body. I see Tanner's eyes widen, but the look in them is not one of lust, it's one of sorrowful rage.

"Where did you get those?" he says, walking towards me as if he can't stop himself. I realize that the bruises from last night's fight must be visible. Jesse hadn't been able to see them in the dim lighting this morning. Tanner traces a tentative finger over my bruises, making me cringe with pain even from the light touch. I feel everything in that moment. I must have been running off adrenaline up to this point but now I'm not sure how I'm even still awake with how bad the pain is. My ankle is throbbing painfully, and I'm quite sure I couldn't walk on it if I tried. My throat feels bruised and delicate, and there's a host of other aches and pains spread across my body.

"My husband did this," I whisper. "Leaving bruises across my body has been his favorite past time for years. I finally was able to fight back enough last night to leave him." Tears start to well in my eyes as I look at the three devastated men standing in front of me. "I never meant to deceive you," I whisper. "I didn't plan for any of this to happen." I take a deep hiccuping breath.

"Pretty girl," Jesse whispers, his voice heavy with self-loathing as he kneels at my feet that are dangling off the side of the bed. I pull the blankets back over my body feeling self-conscious at their continued horrified inspection of my body.

I take his face in one of my hands, my other hand keeping a strong grip on the blanket pulled up to my chin. "I've been trying to tell you. I'm so sorry," I whisper.

"How long has this been going on?" asks Tanner in a hoarse voice.

"For three years," I say bitterly. A thick silence descends over the room.

"I'm going to kill him," says Tanner in a deadly voice as he goes to leave the room. Jensen grabs him roughly by the arm causing Tanner to lash out and strike him across the face.

"Mother fu…," snarls Jensen as he curses in pain.

"If your husband is responsible for all of that, why is he on tv right now begging for your return?" snarls Jensen, looking up at me while holding his cheek where he was just hit.

I give a little gasp. "What are you talking about?" I ask, my mind having difficulty comprehending Gentry's level of obsession that he would do something like that and risk tarnishing his family's perfect name. Jensen strides across the room and grabs the changer off the nightstand next to the bed. I can feel the confusion radiating off of him. He flicks on the television that hangs on the wall and we all turn towards it as Jensen flips to the local news. A newscaster is standing in front of the City Hall. I'm astonished to see Gentry behind him standing in front of a podium that's been set up in front of the building. Gentry is standing in a sharp suit and tie that would look polished if it weren't for the fact that his face is a kaleidoscope of blacks and blues from my efforts last night. I feel a perverse sense of pleasure of seeing evidence of my small victory.

"Is that from you?" asks Jesse, a proud gleam in his eyes. I nod, unable to take my eyes off the screen as the camera switches from the reporter to Gentry.

"Last night at approximately 4:30am my wife and I were the victim of a home invasion. My wife was viciously dragged from my bed by one assailant while another made sure I wasn't able to follow," he says, gesturing at his face. "I'm asking for the public's help in finding my wife. She is immeasurably precious to me and is my whole world," he says in what sounds like a broken voice. "I will pay any price to get her back," he says, his voice choking with what I know are fake tears. As he speaks the screen flashes to a picture of us on our wedding day. I see Tanner turn away from the screen as if he's unable to look at my picture.

The screen cuts back to Gentry as he begins to answer

questions, but I'm no longer paying attention. It's never going to end. I'm never going to escape him.

"I have to go back," I whisper forlornly, not comprehending what other options I have now that Gentry has made this into what is sure to be a national story.

"That's not happening," says Jesse fiercely, standing up and grabbing his phone from off a table. "Pull the sheet down," he says as he presses a button on his phone and turns it towards me.

"What are you doing?" I ask, pulling the sheet up higher.

"We need proof of what he's been doing."

"Nothing is going to work. Don't you think that I would have left the first time that it happened if I was able to?" I ask in a forlorn voice.

There's silence and I see the guys exchange glances. My heart drops. "You think I just stayed?" I choke out. They look at each other again and their silence says everything.

"I'm not weak," I whisper, remembering the strength that I was able to come up with last night.

Jesse strokes my face but remains quiet. I stare impassively at the tv screen as the story about me continues to run. Jesse starts taking pictures of my injuries, and I just let him. I'm suddenly exhausted, all the action of the night before hitting me at once. I'm painfully aware of all the aches and bruises covering my body.

After Jesse is done taking pictures, I politely ask them to leave so I can rest.

"You have a lot to explain..." begins Jensen. I wave him away. "I don't owe you anything more right now. I understand that you have a lot of questions, but the bottom line is that I made a horrible mistake three years ago, and I've had to live with that mistake since that time. I have more than paid my dues. I will answer whatever questions you have after I rest. If it wasn't clear by the bruises covering my body and

Gentry's black eye, I went through a lot last night trying to finally make him apart of my past. Please leave."

Jensen looks at me, an indecipherable look in his eye before he storms out of the room. Tanner's been looking out the window for the last ten minutes, a frustrated and pained look on his face. He starts to walk out but stops in the doorway and looks back at me. "Was he why you never came?" he asks.

I give a low bitter laugh that's filled with all the pain of my memories. "No," I answer. "That's a story for another day."

Tanner blanches at the sorrow in my voice and then walks from the room. Jesse sits on the bed next to me, his eyes locked on the television screen which is showing another picture of Gentry and I on our wedding day.

"I always used to picture you in a wedding dress. But in those dreams, you were walking down the aisle to where I was waiting for you," he says in a broken voice. He stands up and brushes a kiss across my cheek. "You were a beautiful bride, pretty girl," he says, before he too leaves the room. I hear a crash downstairs and I jump. Shouting begins but I make no move to go downstairs and intervene. I want them to have a little taste of all that I've been through.

I weep silent tears. They stream down my face, soaking the sheets that I still have pulled up to my chin. I can't help but watch the highlight reel of Gentry and I's life together. Each picture that they splash across the television screen holds a different memory than the one portrayed, memories filled with immense suffering.

"I'm not yours anymore," I whisper fervently as I stare at the screen. I wish I really believed that.

2
THEN

ARIANA

"I'm giving you a ride," Jensen says gruffly after I get out of my last class of the day.

The way he says it gives no room for argument and I give him a look to tell him I don't appreciate his tone. I look around for Tanner. We had discussed that I would be spending the afternoon with Tanner before the guys' practice, but he's nowhere to be found. I ignore the hallway full of students who months after I started school, still follow my every move because of my friendship with them, the Sounds of Us, or as Amberlie likes to call them, "The Three."

"Where's Tanner?" I ask, while obediently following Jensen out to the parking lot where his black Escalade waits for us. He opens the door and helps me inside before answering.

"Tanner's father unexpectedly came into town. Tanner is dealing with him."

I immediately start worrying about Tanner with Jensen's pronouncement. From what I've heard, Tanner's father isn't that great of a person. Something that Jensen and Tanner both have in common. "Will he be alright?" I ask, turning to look at Jensen who has a stressed look on his face.

"Baby, he'll let us know if he needs anything. Don't worry," Jensen says, and I try to relax in the plush leather seat. We drive for twenty minutes and I realize that I have no idea where we're going.

"This isn't the part where you tell me you're taking me somewhere to kill me, is it?" I ask, only half joking.

Jensen scoffs and then clears his throat. "I'm taking you to my house," he says, and my eyebrows shoot through my forehead. "Is that okay?" he asks hesitantly.

"Sure," I say, staring out my window as we pull into another neighborhood of mansions. All three of the guys are beyond wealthy, but while much of Jesse's neighborhood could still pass as a regular suburban neighborhood, there's no mistaking Jensen's for anything but a neighborhood for the upper class. We pass mansion after mansion, each one bigger than the one before. We get to the end of the street and Jensen pulls into the driveway of a house that looks like it's made up entirely of glass. A giant glass house. You somehow can't see inside the house despite the floor to ceiling windows, but a shiver runs down my spine because it feels like people are watching us from inside.

Besides the one story about how he fell in love with music, I haven't heard much about Jensen's family. Looking at this cold, foreboding house though, I'm not sure I want to. Jensen pulls into a garage that's made of the same glass material as the house and is big enough to fit at least ten cars. I see a few sports cars and a minivan parked next to us. Jensen turns off the car and lets out a big sigh.

"I haven't been honest with you about today," he says. I look at him in surprise, not sure what's about to come out of his mouth. "One of the guys usually comes home with me if I have to come home at all. Things aren't good right now. I promise nothing will happen to you, it's just that everyone behaves better if there's company." He sighs again as I absorb everything he just said. "Fuck," he yells, hitting the steering wheel and making the horn sound. "I'm a selfish prick," he says to me, finally turning to look at me.

I'm nervous. But I can't imagine anything being worse in Jensen's house than what can be found in my trailer so I'm up for the task...even if Jensen was being a selfish prick in taking me here without saying anything.

Jensen gets out of the car and opens the door for me. He grabs my hand to pull me into the house with him. A nervous flutter takes over my stomach at our contact. Ever since our brief kiss Jensen has been standoffish with me. I soak up the contact with him now.

We walk into the house through the garage entrance. It's silent with the exception of the sounds of a game playing somewhere in the house. I let out a sigh of relief when we don't see anyone as he leads me up the stairs. The long hallway we walk down is full of closed doors which somehow seem menacing. We're about to the end of the hallway when we finally pass a door that's open. I happen to peer through the door as I walk by, unable to control my curiosity. It's done up like a teenage girl's room, with light pink walls and posters filled with actors and various music groups on the walls. There's dirty laundry on the floor, and the bed is unmade.

"I didn't know you had a sister," I tell Jensen. He glares at the offending door, a dash of pain in his gaze as he prowls to it and slams it shut.

"I had a sister," he says, before grabbing my hand and pulling me forward past a few more doors until we get to what I guess is his room. My mind is full of questions as I gaze around his room, but I hold them all in knowing that out of the three of them, Jensen is the most closed off. He has to decide to tell you something, you can't force him.

Unlike his sister's room, Jensen's room is devoid of any

character. His room could literally be anyone's room. The walls are completely bare, his king bed is made with what looks like military precision, there's nothing on the floor. It's a blank slate. Even the colors in the room are plain-all greys and beiges that blend into the wall color. Jensen closes the door behind us and then hops up onto his bed and lays back with a sigh of relief.

"I hate it here," he says to me quietly.

"Why didn't we go to Jesse's house or even the library then?" I ask, getting up on the bed and laying on my back as well to stare up at the ceiling.

"My dad made a rule that he'll only continue to support me if I come home every day for at least a few hours until I graduate," he says in an angry voice. "Since we need him to keep helping fund the band, it's a necessary evil." He takes a small breath as if he's trying to gain courage and then he continues on. "I come home for my mom too, just to make sure she's alright. She hasn't been the same since Maddie died."

My heart clenches at the hint of vulnerability in his tone as he talks. It's so unlike everything that I've known about Jensen before this.

"I guess we should do our homework before dinner and band practice," he says with a huff, sitting up and grabbing his bag from where he threw it. I reluctantly get out my bag and start trying to work on my calculus homework, "trying" being the operative word.

Jensen has scooted back towards the headboard of the bed and is writing in a spiral, meaning that he's actually writing song lyrics and not working on homework. I'm itching to see what he's creating but again I control myself and continue to meddle through the mess of numbers in my book. I've always been a good student with the exception of math and I'm afraid that calculus might be the final nail in my math coffin. I finally throw my book down and flop backwards onto the bed, moaning in frustration.

"What's wrong?" Jensen asks, cracking the first smile I've seen since he met me after school.

"I'm going to fail math," I sigh, pointing dejectedly at my math homework which is now strewn across the bed. He picks it up and immediately starts to erase and fix things.

"What are you doing?" I ask, sitting up.

"Helping you," he mutters.

"It's not very helpful if you just do it for me," I retort. "And are you even good at calculus?" I ask suspiciously, considering I've never seen the guys actually do homework. He rolls his eyes at me and pats the space next to him. I ungracefully scoot to sit by him.

Over the course of the next hour, Jensen has me wondering what else the guys are hiding since I'm pretty sure that Jensen is actually a mathematician or some kind of genius. In sixty minutes, he's managed to explain an easy way to do all the problems, something that my teachers have failed to do since elementary. This side of him unfortunately has me liking him even more. Who knew I was attracted to the smart guys?

I glance at him out of the corner of my eye. "What?" he asks, not looking away from the song lyrics he's working on again now that I've finally learned how to do my math homework.

"You're kind of a nerd," I say with a grin. He rolls his eyes, but I can see the smile that he's trying to hold back and the fact that his cheeks are blushing a bit.

We work steadily for another thirty minutes until my curiosity wins out. "Can I see what you're working on?" I finally ask, holding my hand out to see his notebook.

"Ya, that's not happening," he says, not bothering to look up. Unperturbed, I snatch the spiral out of his hand. He looks up at me shocked before suddenly launching himself at me.

I'm so surprised that I end up on my back, holding the spiral over my head while he holds himself up on top of me.

The playful moment quickly spirals into more. Jensen's green eyes hold a lustful longing as they gaze into mine. I can't take my eyes away from his and as I watch, his face begins to descend towards mine. Our lips are just about to touch when a voice sounds in the room.

"Jensen stop fucking around and come help your mother with dinner," says the voice and I sit up so suddenly that I bang my head straight into Jensen's head so hard that I see stars.

"Ow," I say quietly as Jensen recovers next to me. "What was that?"

"My father," Jensen says with a sigh. "Maybe you should stay up here."

"Not a chance," I tell him, sliding off the bed and holding out my hand. When he looks at me, it's like he's seeing me for the first time. Like there's something about me that has changed in the hour we've been in his bedroom. His hand is shaking as he reaches out to grab mine. I wonder what could be so bad that this strong, beautiful man is filled with so much fear. I guess I'm about to find out.

I open the door, and we start to walk down the long hallway. Halfway down the hallway, Jensen seems to find himself again. His strides become less tentative and he begins to lead me. We walk down the stairs and through a few perfectly decorated living rooms, each one more lavish than the rest. Why would anyone need this many living rooms? I make a note to ask Jensen later on.

We finally get to the entrance of the kitchen, and Jensen takes a deep breath before dragging me with him into the room. There's a tiny blonde woman stirring something on the stove that smells delicious. She doesn't notice us come in, and Jensen lets go of my hand to slowly approach her.

"Mom," he says softly, and she drops her spoon with a

loud splash as she whirls around, her hand over her heart in fear. It's an odd reaction and the uneasiness I had been trying to push aside on our journey down from Jensen's room rears its ugly head.

"Oh, it's you," she says in a high-pitched girly voice as she looks adoringly up at Jensen. "How was school?" she asks, pulling him into a hug that looks a bit awkward since Jensen towers over her. I can't see any similarities between her and Jensen. Everything about her is fragile and almost bird-like. And she looks young. More like a sister than a mother, but maybe that's a benefit of being rich...you stay forever young.

She starts to say something else, her hand stroking down Jensen's arm, but he cuts her off quickly. "Mom, I want you to meet someone," he says, turning towards me and gesturing me forward.

"Oh," she practically squeaks as I notice she pulls her hand quickly away from Jensen. "I didn't know we had company." She sees me and her eyes widen a bit as she stares at me. "A girl..." she says, as if she's stating something novel. I look down at my clothes, making sure I do in fact still look like a girl.

Jensen pulls me forward and wraps his hand around my waist. His mother's eyes somehow get even wider, and I get more uncomfortable. I was under the impression he brought someone home with him every day, but maybe it's just been Tanner and Jesse. She's looking at me like she's never seen a girl before.

"Hi Mrs. Reid," I say, holding out my hand with the hope that I can turn this interaction around. She stares at my hand like it's poisoned before a cough from Jensen seems to move her into action. Instead of shaking my hand, she grabs me into an awkward hug that turns me into the squeaker. I freeze for a second, shocked at the turn of events, and then I pat her back uncomfortably. The hug lasts for far too long, and I'm about to try and retract myself when I feel her body start to shake and I realize that she's crying. I look at Jensen in panic. He has a "kill me now" look on his face and he hurries to my rescue, softly pulling his mother off of me.

She's practically hysterical, crying so hard that her mascara is dripping down her face. "I'm sorry," she sobs, not taking her eyes off of me.

"Mom, why don't you go get ready for dinner, and I'll finish this up. Beef stroganoff, right?" he says, talking to his mother in a soothing voice. Watching him I realize that this is a practiced move for him, something he must have had to do quite often.

His mother shuffles out of the room, still crying. Jensen and I stare after her for a moment before he turns to the stove and starts stirring things.

"Can you get some mushrooms out of the fridge?" he asks after he tastes one of the dishes. I nod and hurry over to the built-in fridge. My eyes widen as I look inside. It has every food you can think of arranged in perfect order. It's easy to find the mushrooms because the vegetable drawer is alphabetized. I pull the mushrooms out and Jensen gets out a cutting board for me to start slicing them.

We're quiet for a moment as we each do our tasks, me slicing and him peeling potatoes. Finally, I say something. "So that was interesting," I tell him, giving him the side eye to see his reaction. At first, he's quiet and I think I overstepped, but then he starts laughing. His laughter grows until it's almost hysterical and he's now wiping his eyes. It's the most emotion I've ever seen from Jensen, and I realize that he's laughing this hard so that he doesn't cry.

"Interesting. That's a good word for it," he finally says, when he's stopped laughing enough to talk. He's about to say something else when the intercom sounds again.

"Lucinda, how much longer until dinner?" a voice snaps. Jensen rolls his eyes and takes a deep breath. He walks over to the wall where I notice a speaker for the first time.

"Ten minutes," he says gruffly. "And we have company," he adds. The voice doesn't respond.

Jensen finishes preparing the sauce and the mashed potatoes for the stroganoff, and I prepare a salad, butchering the vegetables since I have very little experience with cooking. He has me grab the salad bowl while he pours the food into some serving dishes. Just as he finishes, his mother walks in, dressed to the nines like she's going out to dinner rather than staying in. There's no sign on her face that she ever cried, and in fact she doesn't even look at me as she passes by. Looking at her more closely, there's a vacant expression on her face that wasn't there before. She must have taken something. She grabs some of the serving dishes and then walks out to the dining room which has already been set.

I glance at Jensen to see what he thinks about this latest development, but his face is totally blank. Looking away quickly, I grab another dish and follow his mother out to the dining room.

I take a seat at the table that's large enough to feed thirty people. It seems odd for our small group to be eating in here, but what do I know about normal family gatherings. The three of us are silent as we wait for the person behind the rude intercom voice to join us. Jensen's mother stares off into space while Jensen studies his plate next to me, his hands nervously drumming the table. Finally, I hear footsteps leisurely making their way to the room. I guess his demand for everyone to hurry up with dinner didn't apply to him coming to dinner.

A man steps in the room and I'm caught off guard by how much he looks like an older Jensen. I feel like I'm seeing what Jensen will look like thirty years in the future. His appearance seems to knock Jensen's mother out of whatever daze she's been in, and I watch as she pours herself a tall glass of wine with shaking hands.

"Anyone want some?" she asks, holding up the bottle of

wine. I shake my head no, but Jensen grabs the wine bottle and pours himself a generous glass as well. The evening is just getting stranger.

The man, who I assume is Jensen's father, stops in his tracks when he sees me. "No one said that we had company," he says in a deep, pleasant voice, one that is intent on charming me, despite the fact that I heard Jensen tell him I was here. "Especially such beautiful company," he continues, approaching the table and holding out his hand as if to shake my hand. Not looking in his father's direction, Jensen lays an arm across both my arms so that I can't shake his father's hand back. I see a brief look of annoyance flash across his father's face before he schools his features back into a charming look and sits down at the table.

"This looks wonderful," he says, as Jensen's mother starts to spoon food onto his plate. I watch as her hands shake as she does so, and I wonder at what this man did to her that has made her so afraid.

Jensen's father takes a bite of food and then turns towards me. "So how long have you been fucking my son?" he asks pleasantly, as if he's asking about the weather. My fork stops halfway between my plate and my mouth, frozen in shock. Jensen has apparently been waiting for something like this to come out of this asshole's mouth, because he's already up out of his chair, about to get in his father's face.

"Don't you dare talk about her like that," he snaps, his face reddening in anger. Out of the corner of my eye I see Jensen's mother drain her glass and fill it up again.

Jensen's father has a smirk on his face. He's about to respond when all of a sudden, we hear the alarm chime and a minute later Jesse walks through the doorway.

"Oh good, I didn't miss dinner," he says, dragging a kiss across Jensen's mother's cheek while slapping Jensen's father on the back good-naturedly. He pretends to ignore the fact that Jensen looks like he's about to choke his father.

Jesse disappears into the kitchen for a second before coming back out with a plate and fork. He sits down next to me and starts spooning food onto his plate. "I'll get you out of here soon, pretty girl," he whispers to me as he starts eating.

At this point I'm beyond confused. Jensen still looks like he's about to murder someone, I can see that his body is shaking in rage. Jensen's father is eating non-plussed, while it appears that Jensen's mother has switched to an all liquid diet of wine which is probably not good considering she definitely took something before dinner.

Jesse chatters about inane topics while we eat, keeping us all distracted until Jensen's mother goes to fill her glass once again. Jensen's father slams his fork down. "For fucks sake Lucinda, you've had enough," he roars.

"Don't talk to her like that. She wouldn't be drinking if it weren't for you," yells Jensen in his mother's defense.

"I'm sure that's what you would love to tell yourself, isn't it son?" Jensen's father sneers.

Jensen leaps out of his chair, his fist flying towards his father's face. Jesse decides at that point that it's time for us to go. "Come on, pretty girl," he says dragging me out of the room, down a hallway, and through the front doors. "Wait here for me for a second, ok?" Jesse asks. I just nod dumbly, too in shock about everything that has been going on in there to say anything.

Jesse comes back outside ten minutes later looking none the worse for the wear. We say nothing as we get in Jesse's truck, and he backs out of the driveway and leaves the neighborhood.

"What was that?" I finally ask as we drive. Jesse sighs.

"Jensen should be the one to tell you this, but he won't because he's a stubborn idiot. But he was in the house when his sister killed herself," he says quietly. I gasp. "Maddie had been depressed for a while, and the truth is Jensen's parents just were too preoccupied with their own bullshit to pay attention. Jensen had caught her cutting herself multiple times and told his parents, but they didn't do anything besides get her on anti-depressants. On the day it happened, we had a late concert the night before, and Jensen was taking a nap to try and recover. He had checked on her right before he fell asleep, and she had seemed fine. When he checked on her after his nap she was in her bed unresponsive. I guess she had taken a bunch of their mom's pain pills. Jensen called the paramedics, but it was too late. His father has thrown it in Jensen's face ever since that it was his fault."

The dynamics I just witnessed suddenly make a lot more sense, and my heart hurts for Jensen and what he's been through. Jesse hits the steering wheel suddenly, shocking me out of my sorrow. "That still doesn't give him an excuse to take you in that situation," he says with a curse. "Tanner and I can usually control the situation, but Carl obviously wanted to put on a show for you tonight."

I don't have anything to say in response, so I just stare out the window at the city lights as we pass them by. My phone vibrates in my lap, and I check it. It's a message from Jensen. "I'm sorry," is all it says.

"Do you think he's alright back there?" I ask. "You should just drop me off near my house and go back there."

Jesse shakes his head. "Jensen was about to leave and head to the practice center for the rest of the night. He'll just pass out on that couch in there, and it will be as if tonight never happened tomorrow."

Jesse pulls into an empty parking lot and I realize we're at the park where the music festival was held. I look at him questioningly. He shrugs his shoulders at me. "I feel like some fresh air," he says with a grin. I shake my head, but I follow him out into the empty field of grass where we once danced and I lay down on the blanket that he lays out. The sky is perfectly clear, showcasing a tapestry of stars that will probably end up reminding me of Jesse for the rest of my life. He turns his head to look at me, and I can't help but feel a symphony of butterflies take flight in my stomach.

He leans in and brushes his lips against mine. It feels wrong in a way to enjoy this moment after the disaster of an evening that I've just had, but as Jesse moves his lips against mine, my capability for rational thought disappears.

It takes me a minute to catch my breath after he pulls away, his blue eyes seem to be almost illuminated under the starlight. They hold me captive, and I never want to be free. "How do I always end up lying under the stars with you, Jesse?"

He gives me a self-satisfied grin. "That's easy, pretty girl. It's the only place where I can get you to open up, where I see behind that mask you always wear. The dark seems to be the best place for me to unleash you. It's where I can convince you that anything is possible, it's the place where hopelessness doesn't exist because the stars do. I'll never pass up a chance to take you out here, to make you forget for a second all the shit that life seems to bring. Out here it's only me and you. And I like that."

His answer was much more than I was expecting, and I don't have a response for him. Instead I inch my pinky finger towards his and link them together. I make a wish on every star I see that I'll get the chance to watch the stars with Jesse Carroway for the rest of my life.

ARIANA

When I wake up, I realize that it's now dark outside, meaning that I slept the whole day away. Stretching slowly, I wince as the full brunt of my injuries hits me. I probably should go to the hospital, but with my luck they would call Gentry. A thrill of victory passes over me when I realize that this is the longest I've been able get away from Gentry for. He had always caught me within a few hours of my escape in the past.

Glancing over at the television which is still on, I'm relieved to see that the news has temporarily moved on to something different than my missing person story. "Fuck," I whisper to myself, not knowing what's going to happen next or how to deal with Gentry's latest powerplay. I can hear pots and pans banging downstairs and I take a deep breath, trying to muster up the courage to face the complicated trio of men waiting for me. I don't think I'll ever forget the betrayed look on Jesse's face when he found out that Jensen was telling the truth, even if it was a skewed version of the truth. And his statement about dreaming of me in my wedding dress, ugh, regret over losing five years of my life will ever go away. Even if my life were to end up amazing, would a piece of my soul always mourn these lost years?

Probably.

Getting out of bed, I walk to Jesse's dresser and pull out a pair of sweats and a shirt, not wanting to put on my clothes from last night. Looking in the mirror, I gasp. My neck is bruised and swollen, as is my face from crying. I immediately start planning for the makeup I'll need to wear before remembering that I won't have to go to the country club tomorrow. I hopefully won't ever have to go again. A big smile splashes across my face and I no longer see the beaten and haunted woman I did before, I see a survivor.

Feeling infinitely better, I walk downstairs, once again pausing on the stairs to stare at the gorgeous men in the kitchen. Jesse is bending over a pot on the stove that smells like it holds something mouthwatering seeing as how I haven't eaten yet today. Jensen is sitting at the kitchen table, furiously writing in a notebook. Looking through the window I can see Tanner outside on the phone intensely yelling at someone.

I clear my throat before entering the room, feeling like I'm encroaching on an intimate moment. When I was 18, I never would have imagined feeling like a stranger with this group of boys. My how times change.

Jesse looks up with an easy smile that falters when he sees how awful I look. It's a testament to the passion of this morning that he didn't notice everything earlier. I had cleaned off the blood before coming to his house, but still...I couldn't have looked good.

"There's my sleeping beauty," he says, quickly recovering. "Hungry?" he asks, pulling a bowl out of the cabinet. He looks so domestic standing barefoot in the kitchen that my heart involuntarily clenches. I glance over at Jensen who hasn't looked up from whatever he's writing. I get the familiar urge to snatch his paper away so that I can see what brilliance he's writing, but under the circumstances I'm not sure that I would want to see. It's probably something awful about me. Almost every one of their early songs that were raging against me were written by Jensen.

Jesse scoops some pasta into a bowl and I eagerly go to take a bite just as Tanner walks in. Jensen and Jesse both look at him expectantly.

"Well?" asks Jesse.

"The label is refusing to delay anything," says Tanner bitterly. "Evidently our idiot agent allowed a damages clause into the contract that would send us all into bankruptcy if we do anything to delay the tour beyond a day." My eyes widen in shock at the sheer amount of money that must be, while Jensen swears harshly.

"Why were you trying to delay the tour?" I ask, looking around the room.

Jensen scoffs and rolls his eyes at my question, and I scowl at him. Jesse, the usual peacemaker of the group, takes one of my hands. "We've talked about it, and we can't leave you. So, we were trying to delay the tour until we could come up with ideas of what to do about that asshole you are still married to."

I blush in shame at his words. Tanner turns to look out the window, running a hand through his hair. He suddenly turns around. "We'll just take her with us."

"Are you out of your fucking mind?" asks Jensen, standing up from the table so fast that the chair he was sitting in crashes to the ground.

"It's the only way she'll be safe," says Tanner. Jesse nods next to me. "I can't leave her," he says stubbornly, walking behind me to envelop me in his arms.

I stare at all of them shocked. "You want me to go with you?" I ask breathlessly, my mind automatically going back to the nights we had dreamed about when they would make it big and what it would be like to be all together on tour. "But what are we going to do about Gentry?" I ask, reality setting in about how he's managed to get me on every missing person list in the country by now. "I'll call him," I murmur before anyone can contribute any ideas. "I'll threaten to tell everyone about who he really is if he continues to come after me."

Jesse and Tanner immediately begin to voice their displeasure with my plan, but Jensen strides over and thrusts his phone at me. "You can call him on my phone," he snaps. And all of a sudden, I realize what his problem is. He still thinks this is somehow an insidious plot for me to get rid of an itch I have after being married for a few years. My chest burns thinking of how low he must think of me, but I try to push it away. I have nothing to be ashamed about.

"Won't he be able to find out I'm with you if I use your phone?" I ask, ignoring his still outreached hand.

"We have untraceable numbers because of problems with fans in the past," Tanner explains. "It's a little perk of being a rockstar with stalkers."

Still feeling wary, I grab the phone and start to punch in Gentry's number. As I'm typing a text pops up on Jensen's phone. *Let's finish what we started last night* blares on the screen, ingraining itself in my mind as if it was written in scarlet red. I pause in my typing and Jensen yanks the phone out of my hand, his face blushing as he clears the screen. He clears his throat and hands the phone back to me. A wave of possessiveness passes over me. Logically I know that Jensen isn't mine anymore. All of his actions the last few days have made that perfectly clear. But he still feels like mine. It also hurts to think that he was probably getting it on with some bimbo while I was getting my ass beaten by Gentry.

I try to clear my head and again type in Gentry's number with trembling hands. I put it on speakerphone so that the guys can hear.

It rings once before he answers. "Ariana." he says in an amused voice. Of course he would know it was me.

Taking a deep breath, I channel the courage I found last night. "I thought I made it clear last night that I wanted a divorce," I tell him staunchly.

He laughs. "If anything, last night's little tantrum only made me want you more," he says. "I never would have guessed you had it in you." I hear a loud crack, and I look up surprised to see that Jensen has broken the top of his chair.

"We're done, Gentry. I'm going to file for divorce, and I never want to see you again."

"Not sure how you are going to do that with every cop in the state looking for you," he says. "There's an awful lot of state resources being put into tracing your whereabouts. I would hate for you to get in trouble for putting them through all of this." My eyes widen at the implication that I could get in trouble, but Tanner's shaking head next to me makes me feel better. I could find a way out of this with them at my side.

"Call off your dogs. We're done," I say, hanging up. I can picture Gentry furious on the other side of the phone. He hates not getting the last word.

Everyone is quiet for a second, and then they all start talking at once. Jesse is talking about how we'll just mail the divorce papers in, Tanner is saying we should talk to their publicist about how to let the police know I'm not really missing, and Jensen is yelling about Gentry. It's the first time all three of them have been on my side since we've reunited, and a rush of warmth spreads over my entire body. I had forgotten how it felt to have them all on my side.

Once everyone has said their piece, we get to work. Under their publicist's direction, I go with Jesse to place a call to the police station at a phone booth at a gas station nearby, telling them that I am perfectly fine, but that Gentry and I are in the middle of divorce proceedings and I went away to deal with that. The publicist figured that it was better to be safe than sorry if they are tracking the phone and can somehow track one of the guys' numbers. The officer that I speak to demands to see me in person and the feeling of dread that passes over me tells me that this officer is one that is in Gentry's family's pocket, and the conversation isn't going to get me anywhere. I hang up without saying another word. When I get back Jensen is about to lose it that Gentry seems to have more sway than they do with all of the resources at their disposal. Jesse shoots me a wink at Jensen's meltdown, and I can't help but give him a return smile. It feels like progress that he's furious on my behalf rather than furious that he's going to be saddled with me on the tour for the indefinite future.

The evening passes in a whirlwind as I fill out my divorce papers and send them to a courier that will be filing them in the courthouse first thing tomorrow morning. Before I know it, I'm in Jesse's car driving back towards the stadium where the tour bus is waiting to take us to their next stop. They are playing at a smaller venue in Charlottesville, Virginia the following night, so we need to get on the road.

Jesse parks the car, checking the compartments to make sure he didn't leave anything since it will be returned to the rental company by one of his staff tonight. I suddenly get very nervous. "Are you sure this is a good idea?" I ask him, digging my fingernails into my legs with unease.

"Never been more sure of anything," he says, his eyes warm and soft as he looks at me. He grabs one of my hands, preventing it from continuing its nervous torture of my leg. "I promised myself that if I ever got the chance to have you in my life again, I would never let you go," he says. "Not taking you with us would constitute letting you go."

My whole body softens at his sweetness. Loving Jesse is so easy. Life would be so different if I could just pick him. Stupid heart. It had to make me love the other two as well.

Suddenly his smile drops, and a hint of panic crosses his

face. "We do need to talk though about the tour." I sit up straighter at the serious look on his usually cheerful face.

"The tour can get a little crazy," he says, looking away from me and dragging a hand through his hair. "We work really hard, but I'm sure you've heard a few stories about the band over the years."

"Yes," I say, and he flinches at the pain in my voice.

"They were mostly all true," he says, his voice now low...and embarrassed. My eyes widen at his admission. I had always comforted myself by telling myself the stories couldn't be true, that they were exaggerated by the greedy media... just like all the other stories of celebrities supposedly are. I mean there had once been a story about Tanner being caught in a hotel penthouse snorting coke off five models' asses. There had been a story about Jesse hooking up with a different woman every hour for twelve hours because of a dare from Jensen. Jensen was rumored to frequent sex clubs in all the big cities...doing who knows what. The stories that had been written about my boys were larger than life. They fit into a world that I couldn't even imagine. It was as far away from trailer parks and southern country clubs as you could get.

"Hey pretty girl, stop whatever you're thinking. Everything will be different this tour. I just wanted to warn you because other people won't immediately know that it's different...that we're different. There may be things that happen that we won't want to happen, and we'll have to put a stop to it," he pauses, taking a breath and brushing a piece of hair sweetly out of my face. "Just don't give up on us. Whatever you see, whatever you're told...just know it's not true unless it's coming out of one of our mouths." He flinches. "Well maybe don't trust anything that Jensen says either until he gets his head on straight. He's so scared of being hurt again that he's determined to push you away before you have a chance."

The words inside me swirl like a storm. What happens if I follow them on tour and realize that it won't work...that we've all just changed too much? What will I do then? More importantly, who will I be then? I've spent so much time wondering what would have happened if I had been able to meet them in California, I never stopped to think about the fact that it might not have worked out at all. Despite my presence, they still could have wanted the women, the drugs, the parties. I mean...what normal, beyond attractive man would want to share a piece of trailer park trash from their hometown. Was I fooling myself that this could work now? Were we all just fooling ourselves? Was this destined to blow up in all of our faces? I could feel myself start to hyperventilate as a panic attack came on.

"Ari," Jesse gently says my name, making me look into those sparkling, knowing, blue eyes that always seemed to be able to see right through to my soul. "Everything is going to work out. There's a reason we're getting another chance. It's not going to be easy, sometimes it's going to fucking suck. But I promise Ari, we're going to get our happy ever after someday."

My heart melts at his words. Happily ever after. It's what I've always dreamed of with them. Looking at the real-life fairy-tale prince that's sitting in front of me, I can work for it if he's promising me happily ever after in the end. There's no story for my life that I would want to end any way but with the three of them.

Jesse opens up his door and squeezes my hand. "Ready?" I nod, ready for my new life to begin.

ARIANA

I've tried to keep it from the guys, but the bullying at school has steadily been getting worse. Once word began to spread that the guys had stopped hooking up with random girls, and that they seemed to be hanging out with me quite a bit, the rumors started to spread. "Slut" and "Whore" are whispered to me every time I'm alone. Things are stolen out of my locker, which is really unfortunate since I don't have much in the way of earthly possessions in the first place. One day during gym, my outfit was stolen, meaning that I had to spend the rest of the day in my sweaty gym clothes that reeked from the three miles they made us run that day in class.

I get notes in all the classes that the guys aren't in. Some of them are just notes asking me for dates, but others...the others are so filthy that I want to throw up at the idea of them. The abuse comes from boys and girls alike. The boys think I must be a good fuck since I've managed to keep the three gods of the high school interested for more than a night, and the girls hate me because they think the guys are off the market. Which really isn't fair to me since I have no idea if the guys are off the market. I mean I am with them quite a bit, but after I go home at night who knows what they do. I haven't heard any rumors of other girls, and they're quick to push any girls away that come on to them, but still...there haven't been any promises made.

A note drops on my desk while my English teacher drones on about an assignment due next week. I don't bother looking at it. I just swipe it off my desk and throw it in my bag to toss away later. I'm never sure who the notes are from since they come from all over the room. You would think that they would have given up by now since I don't open them anymore.

The bell rings and I hustle out of class. I have to talk to my calculus teacher about an extra credit assignment, and I have to do it before my next class starts. I'm almost to class when an arm lands in front of me and a hard body pushes me against the lockers.

"Where are you off to in such a hurry?" comes the gruff voice of one of my frequent harassers. Tyler Bradshaw. He's the school's starting quarterback and would be the school's golden boy if everyone wasn't so obsessed with the resident rockstars. He brushes his nose against the side of my face, and I shiver in disgust. He's done this enough for me to know that it's best if I don't move. As long as I let him say whatever he wants to say without giving him a reaction he usually gets frustrated and gives up. I'm not sure how he manages to time our interactions to when the guys are nowhere to be found, but he's quite good at it.

"When are you going to let me take you out, sweet thing?" he asks. He's a good-looking guy with his dirty blonde hair and piercing brown eyes. In the past I would have been shocked and awed if a guy like him paid me any attention. It kind of ruins the appeal however when you know someone is just paying you attention because they want in your pants because they think you're an easy lay. His hand slowly descends down my neck and I start to get worried, he's never gone so far before. It keeps on going until he's stroking the skin right above my bra.

That's when I start to struggle. "Get away from me," I spit at him as I try to move out of his arms. Flashbacks of the times my stepfather has gotten this close to me rip through my mind making me feel nauseous and desperate.

I hear a whistle, and he abruptly drops his hands and steps away from me. He gives me a knowing wink before he jogs away leaving me by myself. The bell rings as the hall starts to empty. I glare at all the cowards around me who are looking away from me. Classy place this is. I see what the whistle was about when Jensen comes around the corner. He sees me leaning against the lockers and a slow, easy grin crosses his face. Seeing him smile would usually make my day, but right now I'm so shaken up that it doesn't make me feel anything.

As he gets closer, he must see that something is wrong because he quickens his step until he's leaning over me against the lockers. It's the exact same position as what I was just in with Tyler, but while Tyler made me feel dirty, Jensen's proximity just makes me feel safe.

Jensen leans his forehead against mine. "What's wrong, baby?" he asks. It's the first real interaction we've had since the other night, and I'm relieved that he's acting normal. We've texted a bit, but I haven't been brave enough to bring up the craziness of dinner at his house yet. I know what it's like to come from a shitty place, and when I'm away from my shitty place, I don't like to talk about it. I figured that Jensen is probably the same.

"Why was Tyler Bradshaw talking to you?" he asks when I don't answer his question. I want to tell him the truth, about everything that's been going on, but I stupidly don't. The insecure girl inside of me is afraid that eventually my problems will be too much, and they'll drop me. I don't want to give them any more reasons for them to see how weak I really am.

"Just making small talk," I whisper, looking away from him as I lie.

"I don't want guys like that messing with you. If you have a problem with him or anyone else, you come to me, understood?" he says, forcefulness in his voice.

"Okay," I whisper. His eyes are wide as they flicker back and forth between mine, trying to read me. I cough and he loosens his grip on my arms. His gaze strays to my mouth and I watch as he wets his lips. "Shit, I'm not trying to scare you. I just can't stand the thought of you getting hurt."

I pick up my bag from the ground, realizing how late I am to class. Then, it's as if I'm possessed because I for some reason stand up on my toes and brush my lips across his cheek. I can feel his breathing quicken. "I can handle myself, Jensen," I mutter as I move to walk away.

With a growl ripping from his chest, he catches my elbow and brings me in close again. With his other hand, he takes the bag from me and sets it back on the floor. "We're late for class," I whisper. He ignores me, pulling me close until I'm pressed tight against his chest. My body starts to quiver in anticipation when he draws his mouth close to mine.

"What are you doing to me? I haven't been able to get you out of my mind ever since the day I first saw you. There's something about you...I don't know what it is, but I want more of you," he tells me.

My eyes close and I shake my head in small little movements. His name falls from my lips in a breathy voice that embarrasses me. I open my eyes again, and his beautiful eyes pin me down, a tight knot coiling inside of me. I know he can see just how hard it is to let myself fall. Even with everything we've already shared, I still can't help but hold a part of myself back.

"What are you afraid of?" he asks, although he already

knows the answer. I'm afraid I'm going to fall, and they are going to hurt me. I'm afraid that he's a player that's way more skilled at this than I am.

"Stop questioning this," he whispers, pulling a strand of hair away from my face. "What I'm feeling for you is new to me, but I'm ready to fight for it." He meets my mouth, wrapping his fingers in my hair and drawing me close in a desperate way that gives me hope he's been thinking about our kiss at the pizza place just as much as I have. At first the kiss is softer than I would expect from him, like a quiet whisper. Then he digs his hips into mine and my lips part, encouraging him to explore my mouth with his tongue. He pushes into me and it feels like he's claiming me, like he wants to claim every last inch of me. My chest expands against his with heavy breaths and we meld into one, my arms locking around his neck as if I have no intention of ever letting go. His fingers shape to the fine contours of my skull like I'm made of glass. For a second, I don't know where I start, and he ends. It feels like we're one being.

It's different from Jesse's kisses. Jesse has from the start always been so free and open with his emotions while Jensen's emotions have always seemed to be buried deep inside of him. One's no better than the other. But this kiss from Jensen seems like I've somehow succeeded in unlocking a part of him that he keeps from everyone. It's like I have won a battle that I didn't even know was being fought.

A throat clears from down the hall, and I see that it's the principal, Mr. Hardy. "Don't you two have class?" he asks, and my cheeks flush with embarrassment. Although I'm sure that a normal student would probably get detention from being caught in the halls in such a compromising position, it seems that the influence of the guys strikes again because Principal Hardy doesn't say anything else. Jensen takes his time skimming one more kiss across my lips, my cheeks, and the tip of my nose before I finally take back control, grab my bag, and hustle away. It's a miracle, but somehow the teacher of my next class had left the room briefly to get some materials and I was able to slip into class with only the eyes of the students on me. For the next hour, the litany of notes and comments didn't stop, but I didn't care. All I could think about were Jensen's lips, his rough words, and the fact that he seemed to like me...maybe even more than like me.

My high lasted until math, one of my classes with Amberlie. She had a disapproving look on her face from the second that I saw her, and I wasn't sure what was wrong.

"Hey girl," I finally said. Amberlie had become a good friend since the start of school, the best friend that I had ever had if I was being honest with myself.

When she simply sighed in reply, I wasn't sure what to do. One thing about Amberlie, she was always bubbly, always on, always happy. Maybe it was a cheerleading thing. So, for her to be so non-Amberlie like...I must have done something bad.

I couldn't ask any questions for the first half of class because of the teacher's lecturing, but as soon as we were supposed to start working with partners on some problems, I scoot my desk next to hers.

"Ok, what's the problem?" I ask. She rolls her eyes but says nothing, pretending like she is starting on the problems we were assigned.

"Amberlie," I say gently. I wasn't sure what to do in these situations. I'd never had a close girlfriend but since I now had one, I didn't want to lose her. "What's wrong?"

"Why haven't you said anything to the guys about what's been happening?" she finally snaps, anger glittering in her eyes.

Now it was my turn to get quiet. This was not something I wanted to talk about, especially after what had just happened with Jensen.

"I'm handling it just fine," I finally tell her with a sigh when I can feel the weight of her stare on me. Right at that moment another note flies onto my desk. Amberlie snatches it before I can get to it and she opens it up and reads it. It's a particularly nasty one describing in detail what the sicko wants to do to me. It gets quite violent at the end, and I turn away without finishing it.

Amberlie looks sick to her stomach. "Is this what they all have been saying?" she asks. I shrug, trying to look like I don't care, but failing. I don't know how I'm going to get the note's crude and quite frankly terrifying description out of my head.

"I haven't been reading them," I reluctantly admit.

"You have to tell someone," she says, her voice rising loud enough to attract the attention of the rest of the class.

"I'm handling it," I tell her firmly again. We spend the rest of class only talking about the problems. When the bell rings, she hurries out of class before I can say anything. I walk to the lunchroom, a knot of dread in my stomach.

I don't see any of the guys in the lunchroom, which is strange because they're almost always there before me. I get in the lunch line, grabbing whatever unfortunate entree I see first since my mind is in a million different places. Someone brushes against me, muttering "slut" as they do so. I'm almost to the cashier, and none of the guys have appeared. It's a little bit embarrassing, but I actually haven't paid for lunch since meeting the guys since one of them appeared every day to pay for me.

When no one appears, I start to get worried. Walking out into the lunchroom, I realize that I have nowhere to sit without them here. The guys' friends only are nice to me because of them, so sitting at my usual table wasn't an option, and Amberlie wasn't anywhere to be found. I guess eating in a bathroom stall will have to work today. I'm on my way towards the double doors of the cafeteria exit when they suddenly swing open, and Jensen, Jesse, and Tanner all walk in.

They look livid, enraged, scarier than I've ever seen them. I finally understand why they seem to run the school and everywhere else in this town. There is a magnetism about them that makes it impossible to look away. The guys walk to the center table, paying no attention to all the people calling out to them. Jensen climbs to the top of the table and the entire lunch room goes silent.

"Let me be clear about one thing," he starts in a menacing voice. "It's come to my attention that many of the people in this room have been messing with something that belongs to us. That ends right now. If I hear about anyone treating Ariana with anything but respect, we're going to make you wish you had never been born. Do you all understand what I'm saying?"

No one dares to say anything. I'm embarrassed and over-whelmed with what Jensen just did, but at the same time I'm in awe. No one has ever stuck up for me about anything in the miserable life that I've led so far. No one has ever cared.

Jensen hops off the table and the guys all turn towards me. I hadn't even realized that they had seen me when they had come in, but I was suddenly getting the feeling that they actu-ally paid a lot more attention to things than I had been giving them credit for.

Jesse crooks a finger at me to come to them and as if pulled by a string, I go. Jensen puts his hand on my lower back and marches me out of the lunchroom. I can hear the cafeteria erupt in noise as the doors swing shut behind us.

"Where are we going?" I ask in a nervous voice.

"We're skipping the rest of the day. Hope that's okay with you, Princess," says Tanner in a sarcastic voice. I know better than to answer. We walk out to Jensen's Escalade and pile in. I hop into the back before anyone can answer me, sensing that Jensen and Tanner are the scariest in this situation although Jesse doesn't look like he is much better at the moment.

No one says anything as we drive. We drive for an hour and a half in silence before I realize that we are driving to the beach. Tanner gestures to something and Jensen turns down what looks like a private driveway. Sure enough, we pass a gorgeous, light blue colored beach house before finally hitting a pristine private beach entrance. The guys get out of the car, and I follow suit. This time Tanner takes my hand and yanks me behind them.

There's a campfire set up on the beach with a bunch of chairs set up around it. Tanner motions for me to sit, so I sit. As does everyone else. The silence between us is deafening as I listen to the waves crash against the shore. I have only been to the beach once before. My mom had briefly tried to get clean when I was 5 years old. It only lasted a month but during that month she had actually tried to do mom things. And going to the beach was one of those things. It was one of the very few unsoiled memories of my childhood that I had.

"Do you know why we're here, pretty girl," says Jesse at last, after it feels like we have been sitting in silence for forever.

"No," I say hesitantly.

"Why did Amberlie have to tell us about what's been going on at school, baby?" asks Jensen in the same menacing voice he had used at school.

I shrink back in my seat, feeling like a fool. "I was handling it," I say, lying to them and myself.

"You shouldn't have had to "handle" that," says Jensen angrily. "Amberlie said you were getting notes with rape threats in every class, that girls have been stealing your stuff, that guys have been touching you in the hallways. Is that all true?"

I pause before answering, taking a deep breath before I do. Figures that Amberlie would say something after she was so mad at me today. I can't find it in me to be upset with her though. "Yes," I say stiffly, not looking any of them in the eye.

"Why wouldn't you say something?" asks Jesse, sounding

more hurt than angry. "We could have stopped that imme-diately."

"Did you not think we could protect you?" adds Jensen. His voice sounds bitter and I think about the fact that it prob-ably was a sore spot for him to feel like he couldn't be trusted to protect and watch out for someone after what happened to his sister.

"It wasn't that," I tell them, trying to sift through all the thoughts in my head so that they make sense. I look out at the ocean. It's a perfect day, cool but perfect. The time I had gone to the beach it had been crowded and hot. Today there isn't another soul around us.

"It feels like we're unequal," I finally say. "You're always doing things for me, buying things for me, driving me around, taking me everywhere with you. You all seem so far above me, and you give me everything...while I give you nothing."

There's silence for a second before all three start talking at once. Jesse is listing all the things that I contribute to his life, Jensen is yelling at me for being an idiot, and Tanner is ranting about "how I could think that."

I can't help but smile, which sets them all off again. Jensen and Tanner finally fall silent while Jesse keeps on with his list of what he thinks are my finer qualities.

"I've never been able to depend on someone before. I'm not used to it," I tell them. Jesse stands up, picks me up, and sits down again with me in his lap.

"Get used to it," he says, holding me tightly in his arms. Jensen looks grumpy and somehow I know he's thinking that he should have thought to pick me up first. Tanner is looking out at the waves, a slight frown on his face.

"No more keeping things from us," says Jensen finally. I nod and lean back in Jesse's arms, wondering if life could be as simple as that. That there could be someone out there who you could trust. That I could truly not be alone anymore. It seems like that could be the case.

The sun is setting. Tanner and Jesse are out trying to surf, so it's just Jensen and I sitting by the campfire which the guys started. Evidently the house that we passed belongs to Jesse's family, so we can stay here as long as we want. Jensen's sitting next to me, my hand is in his lap, and he's absentmindedly stroking it.

"We probably should talk about the other night," he says. "I'm sure Jesse told you the basic story."

"He did," I tell him, sitting up straighter. "But I would never tell anyone."

He looks over at me and gives me a sad smile. "Baby, I trust you." He looks out at the guys surfing. "I trust those two idiots too. You guys are the only ones that I trust to know me."

It feels like I'm about as far away as a person can get from knowing him, but I don't argue with him.

"I still have nightmares about walking in and seeing her. I still can't believe that somehow, I missed the signs of how bad she was. I had been spending all my time trying to grow the band. I didn't pay attention when her boyfriend broke up with her or when my mother said that alcohol had been disappearing from the liquor cabinet. I didn't pay attention to the fact that she was partying every night and coming back high and drunk. Or at least I tell myself I didn't notice, but I obviously did since I can make a list like that," he says with a sarcastic laugh.

I don't offer any platitudes or try and tell him that it's okay, because I know that nothing will make it okay for him. Time might help him not to hurt as bad, but it would never help him to forget.

"Sometimes I feel like I'm never going to be a whole person again," he says as he pokes the fire and moves around some of the firewood. "You know what's fucked up about afterwards too, after my dad beat the shit out of me and my mom told me that she would never forgive me right before she tried to drink herself to death. It's fucked up that one of our best songs came from that time. That I'm going to be rich someday because my sister killed herself."

I think about some of the songs that I've heard them play recently. Jensen's clever with his lyrics. They're framed in a way that could apply to a lot of different situations. But there are a few... "Confessions in the Dark," I whisper. It's one of my favorite songs of theirs. It's dark and dreamy. At first glance you think it's about the pain of a lost love, but now I can see that it's a song about guilt. About feeling like you're so ashamed that the only way you can get out your feelings is when no one can see you.

Jensen's looking at me now. It's one of those looks that feels like whatever is between us has changed. It feels like I'm always moving to different levels with these boys. I wonder just how many levels there are.

"Ya," he says. "Confessions in the Dark is the one I wrote. How did you know?"

"Because I know what it's like to feel ashamed of your pain. And that's the song that made me know that you did too."

"Baby, sometimes it feels like you were made for me," he finally says after a moment. I take his hand and brush my lips against it, trying to offer some form of comfort.

We don't really say anything else the rest of the night. Even after Tanner and Jesse come back it's like we all just need the silence. We need to understand what's happening between us all.

No one ever picked on me at school again after that day.

5
NOW

ARIANA

Jesse holds my hand as we walk to the set of enormous buses that the Sounds of Us travels with. I expect the two huge tour buses where the band and some of the road crew stay, but I wasn't prepared for what seems like a million other smaller buses and vans that Jesse explains hold more of the crew, the equipment, and all the pieces that make up their tour. This tour is their biggest one ever and just looking around, it appears it takes a small city worth of people to keep it running.

We're just about to step into the tour bus that's exclusively for the band when we hear our names called. Turning around I see Tanner jogging towards us. He looks like he just got done working out because he's wearing a faded Sounds of Us tank top and a loose pair of shorts. I can't help but think of the first time I saw Jensen and Tanner in workout clothes...and then what was under those clothes. Their bodies were even better now judging by the fact that I had seen lots of Jesse in our multiple romp sessions, and I had seen Tanner's chest when he ripped off his shirt during his perfor-

"Jesse, Miranda needs you to look over some contracts," he says once he gets to us. I look over at Jesse questioningly. He groans in disappointment.

"She's the new rep from the label," he says. "She's here to oversee the tour, make sure that we behave, all that fun stuff."

"Isn't that your manager's job?" I ask.

"She's basically our label appointed manager," he explains. "We found out our last one was skimming some money from us, so we've been without one for a few months. But it's impossible to be without one on tour, so Miranda's our interim one for the moment."

I nod thinking that all makes sense. Jesse pulls me in for a kiss. "I really wanted to christen the bus with you," he says with a wink, pulling away and starting to walk backwards. "Don't do anything I wouldn't do," he yells at Tanner before he turns and starts jogging towards the door that leads inside the stadium.

"Princess," says Tanner, mockingly bowing low and gesturing to the bus. "Ladies first."

Looking closer, I can see that his body's at least twice as toned as it was in high school and I have trouble moving at first since I'm drooling over the parts I can see.

Tanner sees that I'm distracted and a slow, sexy look spreads over his face. "See something you like, princess?" he says, and I'm transported to the living room with Gentry when he said almost the same thing.

Tanner must see my face change because he stops joking around and he puts his hand softly on my back and leads me into the bus.

I gasp when I get to the top of the stairs because it feels like I've stepped into an episode of MTV Cribs. There's a lounge area in the front of the bus that has expensive looking black, leather couches on either side of the wall, and there's a fancy light fixture running down the middle that almost looks like a chandelier. All of the colors are silver, black, and grey making the space look more like an expensive nightclub than a bus. Tanner explains how when the bus is parked there's a slide that pushes out one of the walls and adds 60 more feet to the living area. There's also a 60 inch tv that comes out from behind one of the walls. Apparently, there's over 1000 movies stored on a master control in the bus that we can choose from when we're bored. Tanner lifts up one of the couch cushions to show me a drink chiller that's filled to the brim with every soda or beer brand you could want. We walk farther in and there's a kitchen full of gleaming stainless-steel appliances including a stove top, a toaster, a microwave that doubles as a convection oven, and extra cabinet space for preparing gourmet meals. The appliances look like something out of a spaceship, and I already can tell that they're going to have to teach me to use them all.

"Jesse's the only one who really cooks, but it's nice to have the option to have a "home cooked" meal if we want it," Tanner says, shrugging nonchalantly.

"I could cook some," I tell him hesitantly. "I've become a pretty good cook over the last few years."

His eyes get a strange gleam that quickly disappears. "We would all like that, princess," he says quietly before taking my hand and leading me farther down the bus.

Next up is a set of four bunks. At first it doesn't seem that fun to sleep on bunk beds for an entire tour, but then Tanner shows me how each bunk features its own mini television, a curtain for privacy, individual controls for air conditioning and lighting, and memory foam mattress. The bunks don't seem so bad after that. They seem amazing actually. Each bunk is a little bigger than a twin-size bed, but just like how the wall in the living room expands, the bunks can pull out to make a queen-size bed.

"Is it hard to sleep when the bus is moving?" I ask, thinking that they are probably on the road a lot at night driving to a new city.

"It's actually easier to sleep on a bus," laughs Tanner. "I have trouble sleeping for a few weeks after we get done with a tour just because the movement of the bus tends to rock me to sleep." I nod, thinking that what he said makes sense.

The bus has two bathrooms, something that the band paid for themselves Tanner says. Each bathroom features full showers, sinks, and toilets complete with marble countertops and three shower heads, including a special rain shower nozzle that comes down from the ceiling. Gentry and I's house was nice, but it didn't come close to how nice this bus is.

Past the bathrooms are some closets and a door. I'm thinking that the door is just extra storage space, so I'm shocked when Tanner opens the door and there's a full bedroom. Just like the rest of the bus, the bedroom is outfitted in black, silver, and grey. There's a king size bed in the middle of the room and another 60-inch television on the wall across from it. There's even two nightstands and a dresser.

I can feel red creeping up my neck as I stare at the bed, my mind filled with the hot moment I shared with Tanner the other night.

Tanner walks up behind me until he's standing so close that I can feel his breath on my neck. "We rotate every week who gets to sleep back here," he says.

"Whose turn is it right now?" I ask, embarrassed about how squeaky my voice sounds.

"Why? You interested in trying the bed out?" asks Tanner with a wink, pulling me close to his body. I blush fifty shades of red which in itself is embarrassing considering I'm a grown woman. "It's Jensen's turn," Tanner finally says, taking pity on me. "But now that you're on the tour, this can be your room, so you have some space."

I look at him surprised, shaking my head vigorously. "I'm going to be as little of an inconvenience as possible. You guys are already doing so much for me taking me with you."

An angry look crosses Tanner's face. He walks me until the back of my legs hit the bed and I'm forced to sit down. "Let's get one thing clear, princess. You're nobody's inconvenience. This happening is the living embodiment of every dream we've had for five years," he says fiercely. I look away from him, remembering the disgusted look Jensen has had towards me since the moment he saw me. It didn't look like any of his dreams about me had been good.

Tanner tips my chin up so I have to look at him again. His eyes warm as he stares at me. "Ari," he says, and the love in his voice makes my heart ache. I could live in the sound of it for the rest of my life. "We're going to fix you, princess. Until you remember what having us love you feels like. Until you remember what it feels like to be safe and adored."

All I can do is keep looking at him. Those silver eyes and the passion behind them entrance me, they make me believe that anything could be possible.

"Ari," he whispers, his voice gravelly and deep with emotion. I know what he meant in saying only my name. The air around us is thick with sexual tension, but it still feels romantic somehow. I know that sex with Tanner wouldn't just be the meeting of two bodies-it would be the meeting of the sum of all our parts: our minds and souls and hearts. It would be beautiful.

He takes my hand in his and kisses my knuckles. Somehow making me feel it from my fingertips to my chest, that fizzle of desire that ripples through my veins. He sits down on the bed, and then pulls me up until I'm standing in between his legs. I felt a drop of sweat slide down my spine and I shiver, the coolness of it a shock to my warming skin.

Tanner lets go of my hands to hold my hips. He squeezes and pulls me closer, and my hands find his shoulders. I feel his thumb graze my skin and I shiver again. His fingertips hold magic; that was the only way I could explain how the slightest touch managed to ignite my skin to flaming. The mood is less frenzied then the night before, but I realize that it's not any less passionate.

His hands slide up the sides of my body. My hands tighten on his shoulders and I itch to rip off his clothing and attack him. "Tanner," I whisper. His mouth is on my skin, my stomach, kissing the path of my stomach up to my chest.

"Hmm?" he murmurs against my ribcage, sending vibrations to my core. I close my eyes, feeling my body turn inside out in a slow burn as he kisses my entire stomach. I know I'm trembling under his lips, but I'm completely un-embarrassed by it. Tanner knows the power he has over my body, has always had over my body even with the simplest touch.

My skin, my bones-they bend at his will. Tanner stands up and I back up quickly, my back hitting the tv that's built into the wall behind me as he slowly saunters towards me. He towers over me. He lifts up the bottom hem of his shirt and pulls it over his head, giving me the most delicious view of skin and muscle. I lick my lips, longing to run my hands and my lips over all the planes of his body. And then I lift my eyes, meet his, and I feel the entire world fall away. He looks at me like a man who knows exactly what he wants. His gaze is sure, his intentions so perfectly clear. I know he loves me, but this look? It's something else. It's a look of a man looking at me as if he sees his future, like he hasn't just followed the path to his destiny-he's run a marathon to it. And he wasn't tired. Not yet. Not even close.

My palms find the wall behind me. It's thrilling, and terrifying. The top of a rollercoaster right before it pitches forward and falls into a steep drop. "Tanner," I say again.

"Princess," he replies, walking closer to me. He senses the fear in my voice, but he makes no move to stop. "I…" I start. What the hell? I loved Tanner. I had for years. There was no doubt in my mind about that. But until this moment, I hadn't understood what that love meant. Where that love would take us. There wasn't a destination. This wasn't a journey.

Tanner looks at me as if it was endless. And I knew I felt the same way. And that was what scared the shit out of me. He was against me a second later, our hips touching. His lips come to my cheek.

"Ariana," he breathes against my skin.

I feel the flutters in my stomach fly apart. His lips move up my cheekbone and he brushes his face against mine. The harsh graze of his stubble along my skin ignites the match that is my desire for him. I'm on fire in an instant, my hands reaching around him and scratching his skin, anything to calm the burn that I feel. My shirt comes over my head and his arms come around me, finding the clasp of my bra. A second later, I'm topless and our skin is pressed tight to each other. He holds me tight to him as he kisses my face, his movements slow. I'm burning alive, desperate to touch him everywhere.

"You're torturing me," I pant. His fingers trace my spine and end at the top of the sweatpants that I borrowed from Jesse. My head falls back and hits the wall behind me.

"You're beautiful, Ari." His voice is reverent. Would I ever tire of hearing the awe in his voice when he admired me? I didn't want to imagine a world where that wasn't my reality. His fingers slide under the waistband of my pants, sliding against the skin underneath. He backs up and yanks them down, freeing me from the last of my clothing. My eyes are still closed, and my fingers still ache to dig into his skin. He cups the back of my head in his hand and pulls me forward, pressing the softest, sweetest kiss to my lips. His other hand traps my hands from touching him. I vaguely become aware of him pulling me away from the wall and walking me towards the bed. A second later, he pushes me gently onto the bed. I open my eyes, laying on my back and staring up at him as he tugs his pants down. I have two seconds to admire him again before he covers me with his body. A flash of fear crosses my mind. He's experienced.

More experienced probably than the other two together if the rumors are true. What if he thinks I suck? Gentry wasn't the best teacher and Jesse is so nice maybe he wouldn't say anything if I was bad in bed.

He kisses me full on the lips as he settles his body over mine and all my fear disappears. I reach my arms up to the top of his back and pull them down, letting the fire spread so it consumes us both. He braces himself over me on his hands and looks down at me with a crooked smile. His silver eyes hold a depth to them that I've never seen before. He leans his head down and kisses the line of my collarbone. His lips follow a path down the center of my chest, between my breasts and to my stomach. My body yearns to lift off the bed as he kisses me. His lips come back to mine as his fingers travel down my body.

When they brush up against me, I moan. I've been on fire since the first brush of his facial hair against my skin and when he touches me for the first time where he's never been before, it's like he's thrown gasoline on a slow burn. My hands are greedy for his skin, and I run them down his front. Before my hands gain purchase on the part I want to touch the most, he captures them in his.

"I'm too close," he whispers, sliding a finger inside of me. My entire body shakes under his as he teases me with his one finger. He lets go of my hands and they immediately clasp his shoulders, desperately. I hear the sound of a foil packet, but I can't concentrate on a single thing.

"If you touch me, I'll come undone right now." I'm struggling to form coherent sentences in my head, such is the state I find myself in.

"I'm nearly there myself," I gasp as he increases the speed of his hand against me. My nails dig into his skin. "Tanner." And then he's inside of me, picking up the pace that his hands had started. My skin splits apart, my eyes burst with light. The rollercoaster tips and falls into the drop, and I don't feel any fear. The guys weren't on a journey with me; they were my destination.

After we get cleaned up, everything feels different. Every look has more meaning, every touch is saying something more. We're so caught up in the little world we just created that I don't even hear the door open, and Jesse and Jensen get on the bus, until Jensen walks into the back room where we're still cleaning up.

"Tell me you aren't serious," Jensen snaps as he comes to the bedroom and sees the rumpled sheets. "This was my fucking week back here and now the sheets have to be washed." His words are angry but there's an undercurrent of jealousy there too.

Tanner flashes him a proud smile, and I of course blush, hurrying to the lounge area as the bus starts to move. It's not much better up there since Jesse is wearing a huge grin.

"Did you have a good tour?" he asks innocently.

I roll my eyes and sit down next to him. He pulls what looks like an iPad out of the seat and starts pressing buttons.

"Want to watch something while we drive? I need to take a nap before the show, but I can do that right here." He hands me the touchscreen and I start to scroll through the thousand plus movies that Tanner had mentioned during the tour. I choose Dodgeball and Jesse applauds my choice before scooting down on the couch and laying his head in my lap. I try not to laugh too much as I watch the show so that I don't wake Jesse up. Looking down at his perfect profile, and then around at the out of this world rockstar bus that I've found myself on, it's hard to believe that this is my life at the moment.

A few hours later we're in Virginia and I see for the first time the machine that is the Sounds of Us. As soon as the bus parks, workers swarm from the other vans and from within the venue to start setting up for the show tonight. It's a smaller venue than the last stadium so there's not as much involved. This is a college town so the band wants to be able to connect with the audience more even though I'm sure a lot of the students were also at the sold out concerts this weekend.

The boys start to get antsy as we get closer to the show. I stay on the bus for sound check since the security company the guys hired can't come until later tonight. I don't blame them for the precaution. I've been checking the news and the story about me missing has completely disappeared. It can't be that easy that one phone call could convince Gentry to let me go when running away a million times didn't do a thing. Of course, it would be the answer to all of my prayers if it did work, and my divorce proceeded smoothly. But I've learned that I just wasn't that lucky in life.

Jensen stalks onto the bus first after soundcheck. He doesn't say a word to me, just pushes past into the back bedroom and slams the door. I cleaned the sheets while they were gone, it seemed the least I could do. The other two come back a little later, both amped up and ready for the show to start.

What's been evident to me from the very beginning is that the fame, the girls, the money...all of that came second to the guys' love of music. They pour their soul into their performances. It's almost as if they leave pieces of themselves behind every time they play. I've always been desperate to find those pieces.

I'm scratching random lyrics onto a notebook when Jesse plops down beside me. "How did soundcheck go?" I ask, getting a bit breathless when he starts to kiss down my neck.

"I missed you. As soon as that security team gets here, you're coming to everything. Now that I've found you, I don't want you anywhere but by my side."

I melt at his words. It helps to calm the insecurity that's always lying near about the fact that they're rockstars and I'm a nobody housewife from their hometown.

He puts his chin on my shoulder and reads what I've been writing down. "What are you working on?" he asks. I blush and shrug, moving his head off my shoulder with the movement.

"Just jotting down some lyrics," I tell him softly. Out of the three of them, he's the only one who has seen me sing. It's something that connects us, something that will always be special about our relationship.

He pulls the notebook from my hands before I can say anything else. He starts to pour over the pages, getting more and more energized as he goes through them. "These are fucking amazing," he yells, making Tanner pop his head out of his bunk where he had been "getting in the zone" before the show.

"What's amazing?" he asks, his eyes pouring over me, a glint in his eye. I nudge Jesse, not ready to share them yet. I've never shared them with anyone before, but Jesse doesn't heed my signal.

"Get over here and look at these lyrics she wrote," he says. Tanner rolls from his bunk and stalks over to us.

"Lyrics? I didn't know you were a songwriter, princess," Tanner says as he plops down next to me, getting so close to me that he's almost on top of me. He yanks the notebook out of Jesse's hand and starts to look over it. At first, I can tell that he's just humoring us, looking because he's interested in anything to do with me rather than really expecting anything.

As he reads though, I can tell he's shocked. He flips through the pages, repeating some of the lines out loud, already attaching melodies to some of them. When he gets halfway, he finally looks at me. "I don't even know what to say, princess. This is some of the best stuff that I've ever seen."

"Really?" I ask.

"You didn't believe me?" asks Jesse, faking that he's hurt. I elbow him with a smile. He knows why it means so much for Tanner to like something. As charming as Tanner is, he's very opinionated about music and has no problem telling anyone when he thinks something sucks. Tanner is incapable of sparing feelings when it comes to music, while Jesse manages to be a sweetheart no matter the situation.

"We need to sing this," he says, jumping up with my notebook and going to one of the closets where he keeps his favorite guitar. He doesn't trust the crew with it so he stores it himself wherever he's at.

He flips to a song I wrote about that first night when I met Tanner's eyes from the shadows just beyond the campfire. It's a song that's all about falling in love at first sight and how there's no going back. Tanner starts to strum a tune and sing some of the lyrics.

"I think it needs to be a chord lower," says Jesse, and Tanner immediately tries a lower chord out.

It's surreal hearing a song I wrote put to music. It makes me feel proud, like I'm actually capable of achieving at least a little of the dream I've always had for myself. We work on the song together for a little bit until I hear the back-bedroom door open. Immediately I grab the notebook and stuff it under the couch cushion before Jensen can come to the lounge area.

Tanner looks at me questioningly but doesn't tell Jensen about my songs when he asks what's going on.

"Just having a little jam session," Tanner says casually as I grip his hand tightly.

"Well save your voice for tonight," Jensen snaps before storming out of the bus. That's all he seems to do lately around me, storm around in a cloud of anger about my presence.

"He'll come around, princess, but you should really tell him about this. Why did you never tell us about this? This song had to have been written in high school," says Tanner, a note of hurt in his voice.

I struggle to put my insecurity into words. "You guys have always been these larger than life figures. It was a bit intimidating to even think of trying to show any of my songs to you. The first time I mentioned that I wanted to be a singer when I got older, Jensen totally looked at me like I was just dreaming, that there was no way that he believed I was capable of that. It just never really seemed like the right time after that."

I can feel Tanner and Jesse exchanging looks over my head. Jesse clears his throat. "Maybe we needed to grow up a little bit. There were a lot of things that we should have done better back then. Things will be different now though. No more secrets."

I nod, thinking that I've made that promise a lot in my life and this time I really have to keep it. Jesse's phone buzzes and he looks at the text that had just come in.

"Shit, we have a few interviews before the show starts and they were supposed to start ten minutes ago," he says, springing up from the couch and grabbing my hand.

I'm still wearing a pair of sweats and a tank top since I haven't been able to get any clothes yet. "I can't go with you," I tell him, thinking I look about as far from rock and roll as possible.

"We'll send someone to get you clothes for tonight, but since security isn't here and I don't want to leave you alone for the rest of the night, you're coming with us," says Tanner, pushing me gently towards the door of the bus.

We walk through the backlot to the tunnel that leads to the greenroom and the dressing rooms. An attractive woman in her 40s, in a perfectly fitted black skirt suit comes striding up to us as soon as we get to the greenroom.

"You're late," she snaps, scratching something on the clipboard she's holding. "Thank goodness Jensen arrived on time so that he could start the interviews." She has a charming British accent that somehow makes her seem even more authoritative and proper. I feel like a little girl in her presence.

"Hello to you too, Miranda," says Tanner sarcastically as he brushes his hair back. He looks camera ready like always as he strides to the empty chair that's waiting for him by Jensen and the interviewer.

Miranda ignores Tanner's sarcasm. It takes a minute, but when Jesse hasn't let go of my hand and starts to lead me towards where the cameras and the interviewer are set up, she finally seems to notice me.

"Jesse, we don't have time for your groupie right now," she says in an annoyed voice while she casts me a disdainful look that says she sees my sweatpants, and she's not impressed. "I was told by the label I could expect a little bit more professionalism from all of you after the last incident."

"I would suggest you not use that word to describe her ever again," says Jesse, and even though he says it in a charming tone, I can see that aura of anger in his eyes and so does Miranda. This makes her take a second look at me.

"What should I call this charming urchin then," she says, gesturing to my clothes.

"Her name is Ariana, and she happens to be the love of our lives. We expect her to be treated as such," he snaps, finally letting some of the anger seep into his voice.

Her eyes widen at his remark, as do mine. I was expecting to be introduced to people, but I wasn't expecting that introduction. I love it.

"I'm not sure that she can be classified as the love of all of your lives since I know that Tanner was caught with three girls backstage just two weekends ago," she retorts. And I know what she's thinking. Artists are known to be passionate. There're books filled with all of the short-lived flings that rockstars have had in the past. I think back to the look in Tanner's eyes when we made love, and the emotion in Jesse's voice when he told me that he loved me. We're different. I know we are.

"I don't think you're being paid to give us opinions on our love lives, Miranda," comes the unexpected voice of Jensen. He isn't looking at me, but I'm staring at him shocked that he's standing up for me. "It's your turn, Jesse. I'll stay with Ari," he says. Jesse squeezes my hand and gives me a reassuring wink before heading to where the interviewer is now talking to Tanner.

"If she's going to be around, she's going to have to dress better than that," Miranda says, once she's gotten over the shock of Jensen putting his arm around me. I'm still in shock at his move and I'm trying not to move just in case I scare him away.

"Be a good manager and go tell our stylist we need a bunch of clothes fit for a rockstar's girlfriend," says Jensen.

Miranda turns red but she wisely says nothing more as she stalks away, yelling at staff as she passes them by. It's a great start to my relationship with the band's freaking manager, and I'm sure she's going to be fun to deal with in the future.

Jensen drops his arm as soon as she's gone from the room, and I immediately miss the feel of it.

"Go get something to eat," he says in an exasperated voice as he once again stalks away from me to what I'm guessing is his dressing room and slams the door behind him. Somehow the moment feels like progress even if it ended the same as all of our other encounters.

An hour before the show starts an assistant arrives with some clothes and the news that I will have a whole new wardrobe arriving over the next few days. I'm not sure what game Miranda is playing when I pull out the clothes for tonight. There's a light pink dress and a pearl necklace in the bag along with a pair of black wedges. It looks suspiciously like something that I would have worn with Gentry, and I wonder how Miranda would have known that already.

I reluctantly pull on the dress and wedges since I can't exactly wear oversized sweatpants for the rest of the night. But I draw the line at the pearls. Not wearing pearls ever again is a vow that I'm not going to go back on.

I get appreciative looks from Tanner and Jesse when I get to the greenroom and glares from everyone else. Apparently, there's another meet and greet at tonight's show and a bunch of gorgeous co-eds have dressed to impress the guys tonight. Many of them look the part of a rockstar's girlfriend and I want to go hide in the dressing room until the event is over. I turn to leave but Jesse grabs my hand simultaneously to him signing an autograph for a swooning blonde.

"You're not going anywhere," he says out of the side of his mouth as he smiles charmingly at the next fan in line. "What better way to control the groupies than to have our girlfriend by our side," he continues, greeting another fan who looks like she's about to faint from shock at actually meeting her idols.

We get past the first few sweet fans and then the groupies start to arrive. They don't care that Jesse has one arm around me. They don't care that I'm standing there. Their sights are set on one thing. Getting in my men's pants. They whisper things in the guys' ears, and they ask them to sign various body parts, which the guys politely refuse. The looks on the crew's faces watching the guys interact with fans make clear that this is a new development for them. It makes my stomach curdle to think about any of these girls touching what I feel so strongly is mine.

I see several pairs of boobs, and I'm shocked at the girls' desperation. The insecure part of me worries that the guys will miss the easy buffet that's available to worship them every night. I'm only one girl, and not a superhuman girl at that with infinite stamina. Can you really go from three-ways to waiting your turn for a girl?

Just as soon as the thoughts pass through my head, I work to push them out. There's no room for insecurity when you're dating rockstars. These girls are beautiful, but they're a dime a dozen. The four of us share a past that can't be replicated. I know these men, and they know me in a way that no one else does. They are mine.

With that mindset I move to the other side of Jesse. I kiss Tanner's cheek and I wrap my arm around Jesse's waist, laying my head on his shoulder. It's possessive and I can tell that it surprises both of them. I can also tell that they like it.

Jensen joins us after a little while. He refuses to look at me, but he manages to turn on some semblance of charm for his adoring fans. A half hour in I can feel Tanner and Jesse stiffen beside me. I look up to see a beautiful redhead approaching Jensen. She's more than beautiful really, she looks like a supermodel. The smile on her face is genuine, not meant to entice but instead signifying that she knows Jensen, and she knows him well.

I can't go over and just try and claim Jensen. We're not anywhere close to that, but I feel physically ill when she comes up to him and throws her arms around him, pressing her ample chest against him. She tries to kiss his lips, and he turns at the last second, leaving a trail of red lipstick behind on his cheek. It feels like she marked him. It feels dangerous to everything I'm trying to work through with him.

I see him look at me out of the corner of his eye, and then

he slides off his stool, whispering something in her ear and gesturing for her to follow him. He leads her to a quiet corner that is shielded from most of the room, except it's not shielded from me.

"Who is that girl?" I ask in a somewhat strangled voice. I'm gripping Jesse's hand too tight as I ask the question.

"Cassidy," Tanner says reluctantly, shooting Jesse a look. "An old friend?" I try to joke even as I can't take my eyes from Jensen.

He's explaining something to the girl and she's beginning to get upset. Her eyes are filling up with tears and she tries to lean in to kiss him again, but he again evades her reach.

"You can't be serious," she says to him desolately, her voice rising in volume the more upset she gets.

"She's been a steady fling for Jensen," says Tanner. "At one point I thought that she would be more, but Jensen never let it get to the next level. She's a good girl."

I know he's not trying to be cruel, but his words hit me hard. It's hard enough to push past the fact that they've all probably slept with hundreds of girls...maybe thousands in Tanner's case...if that's even possible. But to think of them actually having feelings for another girl, when I've loved only them since I've met them. It's heart-wrenching. It sucks.

I turn my head when she flings herself at him again, burying her head into his chest as she softly sobs. He catches my eye while he strokes her hair and I know he can see everything I'm feeling. I see yearning and anguish and that bottomless darkness in his eyes, and something in my chest feels like it's melting. Is the yearning for her? Is he sad because this is goodbye, because he doesn't think I'm worth it? What if I'm not worth it?

I turn my attention back to Jesse and Tanner who are still signing autographs and greeting VIPs. "I'm going to grab something to eat," I tell Jesse warily, and this time he doesn't object. He kisses me, not caring at all about the jealous looks or the sighs from his fans. It's a kiss just for me. "Meet me in my dressing room after you eat?" he asks.

It seems like an innocent question, but there's a fire in his eyes that makes me know that it's far from that. "You can count on it," I whisper as I walk away aware of Jesse and Tanner's eyes on my ass as I do so.

Like the two concerts before this, there's a spread of food laid out that happens to feature all of the guy's favorites food. But this time I notice that there's a sprinkling of my favorite foods: Fried pickles, teriyaki chicken and rice...brownies with pecans. I almost cry as I look at the food because I know somehow, they had those brought in for me. Even after all these years they haven't forgotten what I like. And I know it's not some random thing because I happen to know that each of the guys hates one of those foods. Hates them to the point where they were probably on their riders that they couldn't be within a hundred feet of them. This is just for me, and it's just another way that shows me we're in this deep.

I fill my plate and am about to sneak into Jesse's dressing room when a resounding slap sounds across my face. I drop my food in shock, my face stinging from the slap. It takes me a second to realize that Cassidy is standing in front of me.

"You bitch," she whispers. Large tears stream down her face and her mascara is everywhere from her tears. "He almost loved me." I don't have the heart to strike her back or even yell at her. I know how she feels. Losing them, any of them is unbearable. She very well might spend the rest of her life loving Jensen Reid. I know that I will.

There's a moment when our eyes connect that I can almost feel the weight of her desperation and the misery she's experiencing. It's suffocating.

And then the moment is over when she's ripped away from me by an irate Jensen who pushes her to where two security guards are waiting to escort her out. He doesn't watch her leave and I suddenly feel much better about beautiful Cassidy and her role in Jensen's life.

"Are you okay?" he asks in a gruff, concerned voice as he reaches out to touch the cheek she slapped.

"I've had much worse," I try to joke, but it's the wrong thing to say as a haze of anger and guilt passes over Jensen's face. He pulls his hand back before it can touch my skin.

"I'm sorry," he chokes out as he walks away once again. I go to pick up my dropped food and I realize that a worker has already swooped in to clean it up. I look at the food still on the table, but I can't muster up enough of an appetite to refill a plate. Instead I just walk into Jesse's dressing room knowing exactly what I need.

Jesse's on me the second that the door closes, obviously not realizing what has just happened out there since he somehow managed to slip inside before me. I sigh involuntarily as his lips brush across my neck, my eyes closing. Each kiss is like lighting a match to my skin. His lips move down to my neck before my head falls back. His lips truly feel like a drug, pulling me under in a haze. He moves up the column of my throat, his hands cradling my head. When his lips meet mine once again, he kisses me softly, slowly. Then pulling away just so our lips barely touch he whispers. "Ari, I am completely, madly in love with you."

I feel my legs go a little weak at his pronouncement and I wrap my arms around him in an effort to be closer and to steady myself.

"I," he says before brushing my lips with his. "Love," he adds, brushing yet another kiss to my lips. "You." He pushes his lips to mine fully. I know I'm trembling. I'll never get tired of hearing those words from him. I'll never take them for granted. I swallow; my tongue feels as if it weighs a hundred pounds. I exhale out a breath. His words fill up some of the empty space inside of me that may take a lifetime to fill. I want to laugh, with relief, with gratitude. Instead my hands move to hold his face. "I love you, Jesse." The words aren't as hard to say as I'd expect now that I've said them a few times. The laugh I've been suppressing bubbles up and releases itself from my lips. I feel his smile stretch his cheeks beneath my hands and we both laugh a little before Jesse picks me up and spins me around in a quick turn.

"I know," he says as he smacks another kiss to my lips before walking and putting me on the counter by the large makeup mirror in his room. My shirts about to come off when there's a banging on the door followed by an accent that I'm beginning to detest.

"I expect you out here in one minute," she orders as she tries to open the door. Jesse moans and lays his head on my shoulder.

"You should have come five minutes earlier," he moans, still slightly out of breath from what had been starting to happen.

"Five minutes is all you needed, huh?" I tease him, kissing his cheek. "I'll have to remember that."

He glares at me before kissing me so fiercely that I lose my breath briefly. "Let's go, pretty girl. The others might want a good luck kiss as well."

A girl can only hope.

ARIANA

We're dancing. Jensen and me. It's prom and the only thought I have in my head is how alone I'm going to be next year. The boys don't usually go to prom, but they wanted to give tonight to me since Jesse had caught me looking at prom dresses online a few weeks ago.

He sings in my ear as I dance in the white dress I found at the second hand store that perfectly shows off my golden skin.

"You can be every little thing you want nobody to know... you can call it love if you want."

It's one of my favorite songs and he knows it. I've been obsessed with it ever since the band covered it in a concert a few weeks ago. That's what a perfect relationship would be for me, that I could be anything, even all the things that you normally would hide from the world. With the perfect love all the ugly dirty parts of you would be treasured just as much as all the rest of you. And I have so many ugly, dirty parts about me.

The thing about Jensen, about all of them really, is that

they also have ugly dirty parts underneath their beautiful exteriors, and it gives me hope that maybe someday I could find the type of love sung about in this song with them.

"Have I told you how beautiful you look tonight?" Jensen says, and I can't help but blush because Jensen doesn't give out compliments freely. He's careful with his words, it's what makes him an excellent songwriter. There's almost never a time when he says something not on purpose.

I feel shy all of a sudden.

"Thanks," I whisper. "You look beautiful as well." I immediately feel stupid after the statement, even though he does look beautiful. He's wearing a black suit that's fitted to perfection with a shiny black shirt underneath that only someone who looks like a model could pull off. His eyes get warm and lazy after my comment, and it's a look that I want to remember for the rest of my life.

We dance the night away, and there's not one thing that goes wrong, there's not one person that's rude. It's all just perfect.

We stay until the last song. The DJ fittingly plays "We are Young" by Fun and the whole ballroom at the hotel the school booked for prom is loud as everyone sings. It's the first time I've ever felt connected to my classmates and I love that it's with Jensen, the person who holds himself away from everyone else at school and always has. We're both like that. Jesse has his easy charm that reels everyone in, and Tanner has his mysterious playboy persona that makes him a challenge for everyone. But Jensen, Jensen has created the perception that he's untouchable, that no one besides the three of us can get close to him. Tonight, he's someone who smiles quickly and often, someone who actually says hi to the nerd that sits in the back of one of our classes.

I can't help but think that this is who Jensen was before his parents tried to destroy him. I want to make it my mission to bring him to life like this permanently. I want to make him happy forever.

T he band had released a song called "Girl in the White Dress," on their second album. On its face it had seemed like a light, joyful song about teenage love and the girl of your dreams. But a closer look at the lyrics, written by Jensen I might add, told a different story. There's one part of the song that talks about all the secrets hiding underneath that innocent dress, that you might think your future lies behind that smile but it's all just a dream. And I know he was talking about that night, how I looked in that white dress, and what that night had meant to him. What he thought that night had meant to me.

After that phone call five years ago, when I told the guys I wouldn't be joining them, that I had changed my mind, that I had met someone else, none of the guys tried to communicate with me except for Jensen. He sent me one letter. It was short and to the point, but it included the line from that song he'd sung to me that one night when we danced under the sparkling lights. The lyrics he chose were ones that carried all the weight of the wrongness of what I had done. It said, "I thought we believed in an endless love." And all I could think after reading it was, I thought I had believed in that too.

ARIANA

Jesse leads me out of his dressing room, and he doesn't stop holding my hand until he's by the other band members who are hovering close to the entrance of the stage. Tanner's bouncing up and down with nervousness and Jensen's pouring over the set list. Jesse gestures to the chest that's been set up just outside of the entrance. It gives a perfect view of the stage. "This is your seat tonight if that works, pretty girl," he says, gesturing to the chest. "We don't want you out in the crowd again until security arrives for you. It gets crazy out there."

I nod, not making a fuss since I love watching them however I can. A face swoops in for a kiss, but it's not Jesse, it's Tanner. "Sorry, I needed a good luck kiss," he says with a wink after pulling back from our kiss. I look over at Jensen who is pointedly ignoring us. He was always the one who needed a good luck kiss before every performance. I wonder who he's been getting his good luck kisses from lately.

The crowd starts to cheer as the lights dim, signaling that the band needs to go on. "Don't go anywhere, or I'll come find you," says Jesse, a thread of seriousness in his voice. I just nod. I don't plan on going anywhere. I watch as they begin to walk out. Jesse and Tanner walk out first, and the crowd begins to scream even louder. Suddenly Jensen appears in front of me, a determined look on his face. He kisses me and it's not just a brush of his lips against mine. It's a kiss that suggests that he needs me to breathe, like I'm his. I'm so shocked, it takes me a second to start to kiss back and by the time I do, Jensen's already walking away onto the stage. I stand there shocked about what just happened. The crowd roars even louder as the band is completed on stage.

Peeking out from the side of the stage I have a great view of the guys, but a more limited view of the crowd. This is a smaller venue. They're playing at the college basketball arena rather than the football stadium, but there's still a lot of people out there. A lot of screaming women as a matter of fact.

A rush of unease passes over me, but it has nothing to do with the women, it has to do with Gentry. *There's no way he knows*, I think to myself. I can't convince myself all the way however since Gentry has always had the eerie ability to find me no matter what the circumstances.

My nervousness slips away when the band begins to play. It's impossible to concentrate on anything else. I expected Jensen to have chosen another night of playing all the songs that show how angry he is about me, but tonight turns out to be a more normal show. Or at least it starts that way.

"We've got a special surprise for you tonight," Jensen suddenly says to the crowd about halfway through the show, walking to the side of the stage where I've been watching the performance. I watch in disbelief as he walks all the way to me and grabs my hand, dragging me out on stage behind him. Tanner and Jesse look furious and shocked, but they make no move to stop him. I'm sure because it would be an even bigger spectacle for them to drag me back off stage.

I flip my hair and try to cover my face as much as possible. It's unlikely that Gentry is at this show or will even hear about a random girl playing a song with the Sounds of Us, but it feels in this moment as if the whole world is looking at me.

"This is Olivia Monroe everyone, and she's going to play us a song tonight." He says the pseudonym with a mean smile and all of a sudden, I'm not nervous anymore. I'm angry. Jensen thinks he can embarrass me. Kill my dream of being a singer once and for all by embarrassing me in front of thousands of people.

"What song are you going to grace us with?" asks Jensen, sounding charming despite the malignant glint in his eyes. I peek over at Jesse whose quick to offer me an encouraging nod and smile. Out of the three of them, he's the only one who has ever heard me sing. Seems like a bit of a jump to go from one person to a whole arena of people, but what can I do…Jensen is an asshole.

Suddenly the lyrics to Taylor Swift's Wonderland float through my mind and it seems the perfect song to sing. The lyrics seem to encompass this dark and twisted journey that Jensen and I have found ourselves on. I grab Jensen's guitar out of his hands, shocking him, and I begin to strum the first chords.

The acoustic version of the song is much different than how it's usually performed, but I want Jensen to hear me in the words. As I open my mouth and begin to sing, Jensen's eyes widen in surprise…and then anger.

I sing the words with every part of me until I get to what's always been the most poignant part of the song. I have to take a deep breath before I can go on and finish:

> reach for you
> But you were gone
> I knew I had to go back home

You searched the world for something else
To make you feel like what we had
And in the end in wonderland we both went mad...

can see that the words have struck true in Jensen's heart as well. Isn't that what he's been doing, searching the world for someone who could make him feel like what we had? The countless women, the drinking, the anger. Isn't that what we had all been doing, just trying to find temporary placeholders to fill the void our separation had left in us? The problem with reuniting, however, was that our pieces didn't quite fit like they did before... and I didn't know if they ever would again.

The last chords fade into the night and the crowd goes wild over the unknown phenom Jensen has brought on to the stage...but I can barely hear them. The only thing I see is Jensen's face. The mixture of emotions; confusion...lust...hate. I can read his emotions clearly because they're the same emotions that I'm feeling. Waving at the crowd, I hurry off the stage unable to deal with what just happened. I should be worried about if Gentry was out in the crowd tonight, but all I can think about is the terrible look in Jensen's eyes.

I had lost him. Even with that kiss before the show, whatever had been between us all those years ago was gone. He hated me and he was never going to get over it. I had to leave. I was torturing both of us by sticking around, clinging to a future that would never happen. I had done this to us. I had ruined everything.

Suddenly, someone grabs both of my arms and spins me around. It's Jensen. I look beyond him, sure that it wasn't time for the show to end. I can see Jesse and Tanner starting on the next song without him.

"What are you...?" I begin to ask, but my words are cut off as he crashes his lips against mine. It's not a romantic kiss. It's an "I hate you" kiss filled with all the bitterness of a love gone astray.

His hands slide down and grab my ass. I can't help but think what it would be like to hate-fuck this man. He'd hold me down, pin me to a wall, to a bed, to the floor, all of his power humming beneath my fingers and zeroed in on me. It would be so good.

He strides back on the stage leaving me breathless. And the show goes on. Brilliant as always, they stay away from their heavier songs for the rest of the concert as if adding any more emotion to the show would tip it over the edge after my forced performance.

By the time the show's over I'm on my way to hide in Jesse's dressing room like the coward that I am. Before I can get there, I begin to get surrounded by roadies and other staff members who are all eager to talk to me about my performance. One good looking guy, Clark, who I find out is the band's agent, sits down next to me. He's good looking with his unkempt black hair and warm brown eyes, but he doesn't hold a candle to my guys.

"You were amazing out there," he says, ignoring the fact that ten other people are trying to talk to me.

"Thanks," I say with a blush. "It was a very impromptu performance. I'm sure I would have been better with practice or even a little warning," I continue, thinking again of the surprise on Jensen's face after I sang that first note.

"It helps that you're beautiful too," he says, placing a hand on my knee. "You could be the whole package."

I'm just about to respond to what I can't decide is a compliment or he's hitting on me, when I'm suddenly yanked off the couch by who I see is an angry Jensen. "Don't you have phone calls to make or something?" he spits out at Clark who looks alarmed at the large man in front of him who is practically foaming out of his mouth with rage.

Without another word I'm yanked towards Jensen's dressing room this time.

"You would think you would be smart enough not to flirt with every guy on the planet when we're the ones who brought you on the tour," he spits out once we're inside the room and he's locked the door.

My eyes fly open in shock. He's actually jealous. "He was talking to me about my performance, you asshole," I snap at him, getting up in his face.

"I should-" he begins, grabbing my shoulders like he can't decide if he wants to grab me or push me away.

"What? What, Mister Jealous? Or should I say, Master of denial of said jealousy - what should you do?"

He growls at me this time, stopping to look me straight in the eye. "I certainly know what I'd like to do," he spits.

"Yeah, what's that?" I bite back.

"Fuck some sense into you. That's what."

Holy shit. I've never been one to imagine sex in a moment of anger. Never before felt the rage and lust cocktail. But right now, it's burning through me like moonshine in my veins. For several seconds, minutes even, as though the earth has stopped on its axis, we stare at each other amid panting anger and craving. We're trapped beneath a ferocious tidal wave of desire; frozen, looming above us, around us, and we both know it's about to come crashing down to drown us in its lustful fury.

I sense the moment Jensen is about to pounce, the moment my eyes secretly, silently, whisper so much more than any words ever could. I want him now. As much as I know he wants me. He reaches for me, his attack viciously laced with dominant desire, his wide grip spanning my waist to pull me into his arms. Our lips meet in a ravenous kiss, pent up anger fueling our lustful want for each other as he grips the back of my thighs to lift me, my legs wrapping tightly around him. Winding my fingers through his hair, I pull and tug in desperation, his hands mirroring my actions in my long tresses hanging down my back. I feel possessed, moaning into his mouth, sucking on his tongue.

There's no concept of our surroundings as we ravage each other, completely engrossed in our deep, anger-fueled need to fuck each other senseless. Turning towards the counter that each dressing room has, Jensen swipes his hand abruptly along the top of it with a fluid glide of his muscled arm, the articles crashing to the carpeted floor with a clatter as he secures me in his grip, his hand at my backside. The erotic display of dominance has me biting his lip in hunger, driving us higher.

Setting me atop, we struggle with needy hands and fingers, tugging and frantically unzipping and then pulling my dress off of me, to reveal my bra and ridiculously tiny thong. They're both quick to follow the dress.

His hands engulf my slender waist as he pulls his lips from mine to attack my chest, sucking deep before swirling his tongue along the pebbled tips. I can't resist the urge to hold his head in place, my legs shaking amid the pounding tempo of my clenching body. "Jensen... " I cry out in a breathless pant. He groans through a final nibble, his husky breaths slipping through parted lips as he lifts me off the counter, making his way towards the brown leather couch.

Dropping me to the couch, I yelp, barely able to catch up as he swiftly unbuttons his black skinny jeans. Bending, his large frame looming over me, he spreads my legs with his strong hands, "Is that what you want, baby? You want me to fuck you? Maybe I should make you beg for it."

"Jensen..." I gasp again, incapable of any words other than his name apparently, closing my eyes against the sheer decadence of his dominance.

"Is that a no? You don't think I should make you beg?" he questions, sliding his fingers along my body.

"No!"

"Then tell me who you belong to," he orders, his tone firm and sexy as hell as he slides his fingers inside me.

"You!" I scream in absolute frustration and need, gripping his wrist in an attempt to push his fingers deeper, my body bowing with desire. I am his. His, and theirs alone.

"You're fucking right, you are," he growls, pulling his fingers from my depths, kneeling down on the bed between my widespread legs to thrust himself fluidly inside. He owns me in this moment - in every ridge, every ripple I feel against my sensitive nerves. I throb and pulse around him. I will never tire of the feel of him. Never stop wanting him. Never stop loving him.

"And I'm yours, sweetheart. Always yours," he whispers huskily, driving us to the brink before we both follow each other off a cliff that signals the start of a whole new journey for us...a whole new world.

One where Jensen Reid is mine.

He's still inside of me kissing the side of my neck when banging starts on the door. It's starting to become a pattern. But this time it's not Miranda or some other crew member telling Jensen he's late for an event, it's Tanner.

"Sorry to interrupt, but we need you to come out here, Jensen," says Tanner. "It's important." Tanner sounds anxious and immediately I'm worried about what could have happened.

Jensen separates from me with a groan, and I immediately miss him, like he's a part of me that I can't live without. He grabs a towel from a stack and pours some water over it, walking over to me. He reaches down to clean me, and I'm touched that this gruff, aggressive man could be so gentle. He cleans himself off and then pulls up his pants. I realize that he somehow remained completely dressed while I'm sitting on a couch butt naked.

I jump up and begin to get dressed as well, a process that Jensen also helps with. Now that he's popped the cork so to speak, it's like he can't stop touching me. After I get the dreaded pink dress on, I let him pull me into his arms. He brushes his lips against mine and starts to make his way across my face and then down my neck.

"Baby," he whispers, and his voice is so full of longing and love, something I've been desperate to hear from him, that I can't help but start to tear up. I squeeze him closer until there's a knock on the door again.

"Come on man, I wouldn't ask you to come if it wasn't important," says Tanner through the door again.

Jensen starts to lead me out of the dressing room. Tanner's waiting by the door with a worried look on his face. "Just you," he says when he sees that Jensen's gripping my hand. "It's band business."

Jensen looks at him before turning towards me.

"Stay in the dressing room. We'll be right back," he says. It's annoying that I'm being told to stay somewhere but the tone he's using is so sweet that I just nod before going back inside.

Ten minutes pass, then twenty, and I'm bored and a bit hungry. I open the door and I'm surprised to see a hulking man with more muscles than I thought was possible on a human being standing outside the door with an earpiece on. I try to move past him. He turns and looks at me. "I'm sorry, ma'am. I'm going to have to ask you to stay inside. We can get you whatever you need," he says in a deep voice that fits the bodybuilder thing he's got going.

"Who are you?" I snap, getting frustrated and a little nervous about the fact that it seems that I'm not allowed to leave Jensen's dressing room.

"Part of your security team, ma'am. We just arrived. Mr. Reid will be by to collect you soon."

Collect me? What kind of crap was that? Figuring that I wouldn't be able to get past Mr. Muscles, I go back into the dressing room, slamming the door childishly to show my displeasure. I get out the phone that the guys' bought me and start to scroll through pictures of tonight's performance that the guys have been tagged in by fans. I feel a flutter in my chest when I see that there's just as many pictures of me performing tonight as there are of the guys.

As I scroll through the pictures, many that look like they were taken just a few feet away, a sick sense of dread comes over me. Gentry hates Instagram, so surely he wouldn't see any of this, but there's enough wives in our town that are obsessed with the band that one of them is going to see these pictures, and they're probably going to get back to Gentry.

I want to curse Jensen, but I can't. Tonight, was a memory that I want to treasure forever no matter the consequences. I performed on stage in front of thousands of people. And they actually loved it. And then I had hot makeup sex with one of the boys I've loved for forever. Yes, I didn't want to forget a second.

And besides, I reasoned with myself, there's no way Gentry is going to get past Mr. Muscles and the crew he has with him. Everything is going to be fine.

t's an hour before the guys come to collect me. They look somber and subdued, none of the boisterous excitement present that they usually have after shows. Jesse walks in and pulls me into his arms. His touch feels desperate as if he's afraid that I'm going to disappear if he lets me go. Tanner looks noticeably subdued as he leans against the wall, not taking his eyes off me for a second. And Jensen...Jensen looks moody...and guilty. I hate that look on him.

"What's wrong?" I ask, looking around the room. Tanner drops his eyes from me, and no one answers my question. "You're scaring me," I finally say.

Tanner finally speaks up. "Nothing to worry about,

princess. Just an over eager fan causing issues. We've got food coming to the bus, and I'm beat. Let's head out."

I know that they're lying, and it sucks. I should press them for more but suddenly I'm tired as well. It's been an emotional day of highs and lows.

As we walk through the greenroom, I notice that there's a party going on. The crew, roadies, and backup musicians are dancing and drinking with what looks like a bunch of the girls from the meet and greet earlier. Everyone calls the guys' names as we pass by but the guys just wave. I do notice that Tanner gets stiff as we pass a table where a few girls are snorting some white powder off the table, but he keeps on walking. The big guy from before is joined by a few other huge gentlemen dressed in black. They walk in front of us and behind us as we walk out of the room and through the tunnel. One of them goes onto the bus before us and we're not allowed to get on the bus until he returns and gives the all clear.

"Was that normal?" I ask as I snuggle into Jesse on the couch. Tanner's rooting around in the fridge when he answers. "We can never be too careful on big tours like this. We've all had stalkers and fans who would do anything to get near us. Jesse even had a woman threaten to kill herself in front of him once if he didn't sleep with her."

I gasp at the story and pull Jesse closer to me. "It's just a precaution, pretty girl," Jesse murmurs, but he sounds distracted, and I can't help but notice that Jensen hasn't said a word.

A knock sounds on the bus door and Tanner goes over to it, looking through the glass before opening the door to get the delivery of Chinese food that their assistant ordered for us.

We spend the next hour eating more orange chicken and fried rice than I've ever seen while somehow watching an

Avengers movie that hasn't come out in the theatres yet. These guys really do live a whole different life.

I'm laying with my head in Tanner's lap while Jesse holds my feet as we finish the movie. Jensen is on the couch across from us and I'm acutely aware of the distance he's trying to create.

"What would you be doing right now if I wasn't here?" I ask suddenly, and then immediately regret my question.

"Partying," Tanner replies. I sit up and turn to look at him. "So, you're not partying tonight because of me?" I ask, feeling guilty.

Jesse clears his throat and I see him shoot Tanner a look out of the corner of my eye. "We wouldn't have partied with the crazy fan tonight. He was just saying in general."

Jensen stands up suddenly. "I'm going to bed," he says, beginning to walk away. He stops before he leaves the room and turns and looks back at me. "Will you sleep with me tonight?" he asks. "I promise we can just sleep."

I feel a profound sense of relief from his request. I was beginning to think that we were going to go backwards again based on his sullen attitude. It didn't seem like a big deal to skip one night of partying, but I had been thinking that he had realized how much my presence was going to hinder his life somehow during his meeting with the band. Judging by the pleading look of love in his eyes right now, that wasn't the case.

"I would love to," I tell him, getting off the sofa.

Jesse groans. "I get you tomorrow night," he tells me. I want to invite Tanner and Jesse to come with us. I obviously have a problem since I miss them whenever we're not in the same room. But Jensen seems like he needs some alone time tonight and that's the only way to make this unique relationship of ours work is to balance all of their needs.

"Of course," I whisper to Jesse as I give him a kiss. I lean in to kiss Tanner next and he deepens it by pulling me into his lap. My heart is racing a bit as I reluctantly remove myself from his lap and walk towards Jensen. He takes my hand and leads me to the back bedroom.

It's the most normal night I've had with them I realize as we stand side by side in one of the small bathrooms and brush our teeth. It's a different kind of closeness and I love it. The last few days have felt like nothing but drama. This is the first time that it feels like an almost normal relationship. If a normal relationship was with three gorgeous rockstars and people normally slept in their super tricked out bus during their world tour. That kind of normal.

Since I haven't gotten any clothes beyond the pink dress set I received tonight, I slip on one of Jensen's t-shirts to sleep in. Jensen doesn't take his eyes off of me as he slips off his shirt and jeans, leaving him in nothing but a tight pair of briefs that leave very little to the imagination. The fact that I don't have to imagine how impressive he is underneath those briefs makes me blush and avert my eyes despite the fact that he was literally inside of me just a few hours ago.

He gives a low throaty chuckle that only makes me want him more. Despite the fact that my body is burning for him after his little strip tease, he remains true to his word and just holds me. As I'm falling asleep wrapped in his arms, he whispers something in my ear. It sounds like he says, "I'll always keep you safe," but why would he be worried about that now? I fade into dreamland before I can ask any questions.

Jensen
Only in my wildest imagination did I ever think I would have this gorgeous creature in my arms again. I don't dare fall asleep because I don't want to miss anything. I don't want to miss how she presses herself against my chest even in her sleep. I don't want to miss her soft sighs or her

sweet breaths. I don't want to miss how she looks totally relaxed and open while she sleeps, so different from the girl who during the day is often so closed off. When my pride finally broke and I had her in my arms tonight, it's as if a door was opened and on the other side of the threshold stood both my past and my future. A future that up to now, I've spent 5 years desperately trying not to want.

I love her. I love her with every ounce of my soul and when I think of the danger I put her in tonight....my heart clenches in my chest painfully. I sigh and rest my forehead against her hair, causing her to stir briefly. I'll die before anything happens to her.

ARIANA

I stand in front of the mirror looking at myself. I've been a brunette my whole life but I'm suddenly desperate for a change. It doesn't feel like me anymore. And the fact that Gentry will be looking for a brunette is just another reason why I should make a change now.

I look at the box in my hand and take a deep breath. I was too scared to try and bleach my hair with a box kit so I bought a box of black hair dye thinking it would be easier. The girls in high school had always had sleepovers where they dyed each other's hair, coming back to school the next day looking totally different. It couldn't be that hard to do.

Taking one last look at the old Ari, I get to work. I've never used any kind of dye so I'm sure I look ridiculous applying it. After I've got it covering all my hair, I have a momentary freak out about how dark it looks. What if I end up looking like some kind of goth chick and the guys kick me off the tour from embarrassment? Taking a deep breath, I turn away from the mirror, nervously counting down the time to when I can wash it.

There's a knock on the door. "Everything alright, Princess?" asks Tanner. "Your stomach feeling okay?"

Lovely. He thinks I'm taking a crap in the tour bus. I cringe, despite the fact that he can't see me. "I'll be out soon," I tell him. "Feeling fine," I add.

"We have to go do soundcheck. Will you be okay meeting us in the greenroom?" he asks. "Security is waiting right outside the bus to take you."

I roll my eyes thinking of the hulking giants that have become my constant companions when the guys are busy with commitments. "No problem," I respond. I hear him walk away, and I give a sigh of relief as I realize it's time to wash out the dye.

I get in the shower and watch as the water turns black from the dye. I stand in the scalding hot water until the water finally runs clear and then, wrapping a towel around me, I step out of the shower and look in the mirror. It's dark and my freak out continues, but I force myself to calm down while I blow dry it. The color lightens up as I dry it, and I start to have hope. I put on some makeup, putting more eyeliner on my eyes than usual but feeling like the dark hair requires it. I put on some red lipstick for good measure, and then I take a step back from the mirror to take a look at myself.

I look good. And completely different. I had always thought of myself as having a girl next door kind of look about me, but this girl looking at me from the mirror is no girl next door. She's the star of the show. It's like I've put on a costume and all of a sudden become a braver, sexier version of myself.

"I can be this girl," I whisper.

Taking one last look in the mirror, I crack the door open and peer out to see if anyone's in the main room of the bus. Seeing that there's no one there, I walk to the back bedroom where I've been storing my stuff, and I open up the closet.

When Miranda conveniently "forgot" to order me new clothes, Tanner had their personal stylist go out and get me an entirely new wardrobe since I couldn't exactly drop by Gentry's house and pack my clothes up. My wardrobe now reflected the style of what a "rockstar's girlfriend" should look like as the stylist had snootily told me after seeing my reaction to some of her picks. The stylist didn't realize that my reaction hadn't been bad, it had just been awestruck. For years I had been wearing pink, pearls, and paisley. I still hadn't fully been able to accept that it wasn't my life anymore. There was no pink in the stylist's picks. And definitely no pearls. The new clothes hadn't fit who the old Ari was, but they definitely fit the new Ari. Feeling daring, I choose a black corset that I pair with a pair of skin-tight black jeans. Sky high black heels with red bottoms complete the look. It's like I've stepped into a disguise, and I've been given permission to be anyone but myself for the night.

Taking a deep breath, I head out of the tour bus, careful to press the code to lock it up behind me. I'm gratified that my new look is a good one by the fact that my security team takes a double take when they see me. I think Johnson, the security team leader, could actually be described as looking shocked by my new look.

"Ms. Thorne?" one of the guys asks, swallowing hard. That was another change. I was permanently stuck with the name Olivia Thorne for the duration of the tour until my divorce from Gentry was finalized, and the guys felt I was safe. Jensen's made up pseudonym for me had stuck.

To the newspapers requesting interviews after the show I was just the mysterious ingenue that had disappeared just as quickly as I had appeared. Miranda had made quick work with the band's publicity team in making sure that I disappeared from the headlines after that next day. I was hoping that I would get another chance to perform with the band, but ever since that first night they had seemed overly cautious about everything without telling me why. Maybe my new look would get them to stop treating me with kid gloves.

The security team surrounds me as I walk through the tunnel towards the greenroom. Tonight, we are performing at FedEx Field in Washington D.C. and the crowd was expected to be huge, more similar to the first set of shows I had attended than the couple of college venues the band had performed at since then. After tonight's show we would be headed to New York City first thing for a set of three shows. I wished we had more time to explore Washington D.C. since I had never been there or anywhere, but Jesse had promised they would take me out in New York City since we would be there longer. "I'll show you the world," he had promised me. I was going to hold him to it.

The first thing I notice is that Miranda is berating the band about something as I walk in the greenroom where the guys have just finished an interview. She sees me come in and her mouth drops open. Our relationship hasn't gotten better and true to form, instead of commenting about my new look, she scoffs and struts away.

The second thing I notice, the guys look troubled. They've seemed stressed ever since they disappeared for that "band meeting" and though they tell me it's no big deal, I can't help but think it's something to do with me.

The band still has sound check and fan meets and greets to do, but Tanner already has a bottle of whiskey in his hands. He takes a long swig as Jesse says something to him angrily.

"Hi," I say, wanting to break up whatever is going on. Jensen sees me first. His face registers shock, but after a moment it just becomes hungry looking. Jesse and Tanner both look at me at the same time and suddenly I feel like a bunny that's about to be devoured by wolves. If the wolves were delicious sex gods of course.

"No," says Jensen, getting up and striding towards me. He grabs my arm and starts to haul me back where I had just come from. "What are you doing?" I ask, stopping us suddenly and almost toppling over on my too tall high heels.

"No one is allowed to see you like this. You'll break the tour," he says, actually sounding serious. I roll my eyes, but I feel gratified at his possessive reaction. He thinks I look good. They all think I look good. Tanner comes up behind me, the whiskey bottle left behind, and puts his hands on my hips while he leans in to me and starts kissing up my neck.

"You're the hottest fucking thing I've ever seen," he whispers in my ear. Combined with Jensen's fierce expression as he crowds me from the front, I'm feeling like the temperature in the room has risen a few million degrees. When Jesse comes over and yanks me towards him, I only get hotter. He kisses me and seems just about to try and take it further when there's the sound of throat clearing from behind us.

"I believe we have things to do, gentlemen," says Miranda, spoiling the fun as usual. Jesse groans against my mouth but pulls away. Tanner grabs my hand though and has me walk beside him as he walks onto the stage where all of their equipment is already set up and waiting for them to do sound check.

"I thought that you guys weren't going to have me sing with you for a while," I mutter as I look out at the vast empty stadium where they will be performing to sixty-five thousand people later on.

"I think we need to save our voices for the show tonight, so I think you should sing some songs while we check that our instruments are working," says Jesse with a laugh. Jensen rolls his eyes when I look at him, but he goes over to the drum kit and winks at me after picking up the drum sticks.

"What are we starting with, sexy girl?" asks Jesse, strumming a note.

The next hour is one of the best of my life. We play through some of my favorites of their songs like "Broken Hearted Love Song" and "Just a Friend." I then lead them through some of my favorite covers, "Turning Tables" by Adele, "Dirty Little Secret" by All American Rejects, and others. I sing my heart out to the empty stadium and a piece of me that's been locked up tight begins to bloom.

The guys are delirious with excitement afterwards, as am I. I can tell that they mean it when they say that I have talent, that I'm amazing. But it seems like there's an ocean between my current circumstance having to operate under a whole new name, and ever being the star that I dream about becoming.

Miranda eyes me speculatively when we run off stage, but she surprisingly says nothing. We get through the fan meet and greet. This time Jensen gently guides me to Tanner's side as the fans start to arrive. I realize why when a group of girls wearing shirts with Tanner's face on them rush inside. They almost bowl us over before security can push them back. Evidently Tanner's personal fan club is based in Washington, D.C., and the fans showing up tonight will be some of the most avid ones we come across.

"Why Washington, D.C.?" I ask as he signs what seems like the hundredth Tanner shirt. He grimaces and ducks his head.

"I may have gone streaking one night when I was drunk here and the newspapers all got the pics," he says under his breath.

I burst out laughing, wondering at how I missed this when I would stalk them all online. It must have been a time when I was trying to go cold turkey.

"I'm glad my pain amuses you," says Tanner, unable to stop his own smile. "I think you should make me feel better," he says in an innocent tone that doesn't fit with the wicked gleam in his eyes.

"And how do I do that?" I ask, my voice somehow growing deeper and more seductive as the mood changes between us.

"I think you guys can finish up, right?" he asks, already taking my hand while Jensen and Jesse groan. Tanner ignores them. I think he's going to take me to his dressing room, but instead he pulls me to a door I hadn't noticed before and takes me up a set of stairs. He leads me over to a floor to ceiling window that looks out at the whole stadium. A stadium that's starting to fill up with people. "Can they see us in here?" I ask. Tanner goes over to the door and after locking it, he flips a switch.

"Now no one can see in," he says. Trusting him that he wouldn't want my naked body paraded all over the news, I let him gently push me until I'm pressed up against the window.

He slowly undoes the clasps on the back that are holding up my corset, sliding it off my body. Tanner pulls away but he doesn't go far, turning me around so it's my back that's leaning against the glass. He presses his forehead against mine and looks down as he starts to trace the skin down to my breasts. Since the corset had so much support, I hadn't bothered wearing a bra and I'm completely bare as he touches me. I reach up to touch his lips. Eyes sparking with dark lust, he licks the tips of each digit.

"Sweet," he says, pulling them away from his lips and pressing them to mine. "Suck."

I groan and do as he commands, letting him take over, take control. It feels so good to let go. I lick him, suck the sweetness like I would him as if he had come—flicking and rolling my tongue between deep drags. His nostrils flair and then his mouth replaces his fingers and he devours me, hard and demanding. I lean into his power, the strength in his chest and his arms as they tighten around me, holding me in place. It's a side of Tanner I haven't seen, and I fall helpless into his control.

"Princess," he whispers, not satisfied until I'm looking

him in the eyes again. This man unravels me, and I can't help but kiss him again.

Tanner

The sweet, unassuming kiss sparks my desire for her, making me feel more alive than I have in forever. My skin buzzes with electricity as she flashes a lazy smile at me. I watch her, mesmerized, as she turns those gorgeous gold eyes on me. She bites on her lip as I pull my shirt off. Playful Ari. It had been two days since I'd had her and I missed her, desperately. I wasn't feeling playful. The swelling in my chest, knowing this wasn't a dream, that she was still here. The knowledge that I can keep her forever overpowers me, takes over all of my movements. I make quick work of her tight pants and her little slip of a thong. I hold her underwear in my hands, and keeping my eyes trained on hers, I bring it up to my face and inhale. I watch her face change. The playful glint leaves her eyes. In its place is heady desire. I inhale her scent, my favorite in the world, and I feel my whole-body change, shift into a familiar place.

Don't get me wrong. It wasn't that I didn't love seeing her playful side. But my heart was burning in my chest, and I had seriously potent feelings for her, feelings that stole my air and changed the rhythm of my heartbeat. In Ari, I found more than love, more than hope and peace. I found my home.

I walk slowly to her, watching the movement of her throat as she swallows. My eyes move to meet hers the moment my hands touch her skin. Her skin. Each time I touch her, my fingers come alive, as if she was the most beautiful instrument my hands would ever touch. I press my lips to her forehead, I feel the heat of her breath on my neck.

My eyes close and I savor this moment, savor being home again. My fingers slide from her arms up and over her shoulders, touching her neck. My thumbs trace her jaw line, meeting at the center of her chin. My thumbs tremble when I watch her lips part. Every single part of her was made perfectly for me. I brush a thumb over her lips and look into her eyes again. They're clouded over with lust. Seeing that lights a match in my veins. My arms move to encircle her as my mouth touches hers. I capture the breath she's about to take and sink in, lips and tongues and nibbles from teeth.

"Tanner," she moans against my mouth. I turn her around, so she's completely bare pressed up against the glass, the entire stadium of thousands of people beneath her. If they only could see the decadent tableau laid out above them. I relish the fact that out of all the people in this stadium, this is mine. Only mine. I crush her body to mine, winding my hands through her unfamiliar ebony locks, diving my fingers into the strands. Turning her head towards me, I kiss her ferociously.

I pull back to catch my breath, our noses pressed against each other. I fill my lungs as I look at her. "You make me crazy," I tell her, my voice foreign even to me. I cup her cheek with one hand while she looks at me, her eyes open and unguarded.

"I don't think you'll ever understand the depth of my feelings for you."

She swallows hard, sucking in air. "I feel the same way," she says. I smile, running a hand down the side of her face, feeling an ache blooming in my chest at having her here in my arms. I want to bury myself in her smiles, in the way she looks at me. On impulse, I bury my head against her neck, breathing in her scent again. I send up a silent thank you to the powers that be that they sent her back to me.

"Tanner," she says. "Hmm?" I murmur against her hair. "I really want you. Now."

I pull back abruptly and seal my lips to hers. I feel her purr in the back of her throat. Bliss. That's what this is. I run my hands up her back, along the line of her spine. She pulls back and abruptly sucks in a breath as my fingers follow along to the front of her ribs, over her breasts, over her curves. I hear her suck in a breath and a second later, she's flipped herself around, her delicate hands on my shoulders, impatient for more.

She runs her hands down my chest, over my stomach. My muscles clench involuntarily. She looks up at me with just the light spilling in from the glass lighting up her face. Her lips are swollen and parted, her eyes heavy-lidded. So fucking beautiful. I can't keep my eyes off of her. My blood is pounding in my veins.

"Do you know what you do to me, princess?" She bites her lip and the corners of her eyes crinkle.

"Show me," she whispers.

I step between her legs and run my hands up her thighs, squeezing every few inches. I feel her skin tremble beneath my hands, and I smile calmly, patiently, at her. Her eyes are burning with lust, their gold the brightest shade I've seen them. I run a finger gently up her inner thigh, back and forth.

"Tanner," she pleads this time, impatience clear in her voice. But I still move slowly, unwilling to rush this. I push a soft kiss to her lips before turning her around, her back to my front, loving the view of her pressed against the glass with the whole world spread out in front of her. I move her hair to rest over one shoulder. I kiss a line over the gorgeous curve that exists between her neck and her shoulder. My hands move all over her while my lips press kisses across her exposed shoulder.

"We never get enough time," I whisper against her skin. "I didn't get to explore all your delicate curves and lines the way I wanted to last time." I put my lips to her ear, nibbling on her lobe. "I plan to do a lot of exploring, princess," I breathe.

My hands move around to her front, cupping her breasts.

Her head falls back onto my shoulder and I kiss the side of her neck, while I squeeze her gently.

"Fuck, you're flawless."

"I think you're trying to make love to me with your words, Tanner," she says, her eyes closed, her chest heaving with exertion. I push the hair from her face as I make her kiss me again.

"Every single part of me wants that. I want to fill your thoughts, so that there isn't room for anything but me."

"And them, right?" she says, a look of vulnerability all over her face.

"And them too," I agree. Ari had always been all of ours. I didn't know how it could not ever be that way.

I reach down for my jeans, grabbing the condom I'd put in my pocket earlier that morning with the hope of this moment on my mind. I always explored the stadiums when we were at new places, and I knew this was the perfect place to take her as soon as I saw it.

"You've filled my thoughts since day one," she tells me as I slide a condom on. I don't plan on sharing her thoughts with anyone but the other two for a long, long time.

She looks back at me, her eyes full of emotion. She lifts a hand to cup my face. "You do, Tanner," she whispers earnestly. I lean down and kiss her, feeling my heartbeat settle in my chest. And then my body joins with hers in a dance that belongs only to us, with the music only we can hear. Every single second is worth all the years of missing her. All the years of agony, of the dreams and the nightmares, the way I yearned desperately for this, for her breath on my skin, her body in my arms, her heartbeat in my ear. Everything was worth this moment. I'm never letting it go.

9

THEN

ARIANA

Jensen's mother died at the beginning of my senior year. She took a bottle of scotch from the liquor cabinet downstairs, and followed that up with ten pain pills, and she simply fell asleep, wrapped up in her daughter's bed in the room that had never been touched since her daughter's death.

It was a maid that found her. Jensen had been at the beach with the three of us, enjoying the last warm days before fall truly set in. I'll remember the look on his face when he checked his messages until the day that I die. It was conflicted, a mix of agony and anger that I never want to see again.

As I stood clenching his hand at the gravesite on a cloudy, rainy day, as the preacher went on and on about how his mother was in a better place, all I could think about was that I was so glad he had been with us when it happened. I was so glad that he didn't have to find her, that he didn't have to take that memory with him forever.

His father had been out of town on a "business trip" when

it happened. There was a pretty younger woman standing next to him at the gravesite today, and I had the horrible suspicion that she was the next Mrs. Reid, already lined up for when something like this happened. Jensen was pointedly ignoring his father, and his father for his part had been smart enough not to approach him.

After the service is over a crowd of well-wishers gather around Jensen, giving him false platitudes about what a great woman his mother was, and how much she would be missed around the community, a community that had ignored her existence for the entire time she had lived in it.

He stiffly accepts their condolences, my hand tight in his. It's like I'm his lifeline to surviving this day. I'm not sure what to do. I'm not sure how to act. So, I just try to be there for him. I've realized that Jensen sees himself as the protector in his little world. And in his eyes, he's failed now twice to protect the people that he loves best.

His father leaves without saying goodbye, his probable mistress following close behind him as he walks away. He never looks back and all I can think is how glad I am that Jensen was able to move out this year from that hell house. Even if it meant that I was all alone without them at school.

We eventually walk to Jensen's Escalade. Jesse and Tanner somehow know that he needs time alone with me, and they drive off in another car.

Jensen doesn't say a word to me the whole drive. We eventually arrive at the warehouse they rent out to practice. I'm not sure what we're doing here, but I follow him silently inside.

Once we're inside he stands there for a moment, looking around unseeingly at the warehouse around us. And then he yells. It's a tortured sound, more scream really than a yell, and it echoes off the walls around us. He picks up a set of drums and throws them, shattering at least two of them with the impact.

Furniture is overturned, pages are ripped, and all I can do is stand there as it happens. He suddenly sinks to his knees and starts crying. "I'm sorry, please," he cries, facing demons that I can't see.

"Jensen," I whisper, taking a step towards him.

"Stay away from me," he spits out angrily, clenching his hair so hard that I'm afraid he's going to pull it out.

I'm helpless in that moment, and then the dumbest words I could say in that moment fall out of my mouth. "I love you," I tell him, meaning it with every breath in my body.

"Don't say that," he rages, looking back at me with angry, hate filled eyes. I know it's not me that he's mad at, but it makes me take a step back, nonetheless.

A look of regret immediately passes over his features at my retreat. "I can't be around you right now," he says to me. I nod and quietly leave the warehouse to give him some peace. As I stare up at the rain-soaked sky, I can't help but think how unfair life can be.

"You can't love me," I hear Jensen say a few minutes later from behind me as he walks towards where I'm standing in the pouring rain.

"Jensen, no." I twist so we're nose to nose and tears well, one escaping in a hot race down my cheek.

"Someone as good as you can't love someone like me," he continues as he comes to stand next to me.

My heart sinks. "I'm not sure things like that matter," I murmur and glance over as he searches the horizon, maybe looking for the same things as me—peace, acceptance, and a place to belong. He sinks to his knees, burying his face in my stomach as he clenches his hands in my rain-soaked dress.

I take in his grief because he needs me to. Together we heal, because there is no other way for us but into the silence where there is love. I love him.

"Baby," he murmurs into me. "I was hanging out in the shade for too long. Where have you been?" I peel away far enough to look into his turbulent, shining, green eyes and place my hand over his racing heart. "Right here, Jensen Reid. I'll always be right here with you."

ARIANA

I climb into the bus, exhausted and exhilarated from the show. New York City was amazing tonight. I'll be glad that we have a two-day break after this set of shows though. I've realized that the rockstar life is not for the faint of heart. While the parties are fun, it's the quiet moments that I treasure. The moments when I'm cuddling with Tanner, writing songs with Jesse, or with Jensen watching one of our favorite movies on the bus. Or when I listen in on the band's practice sessions when they're trying out new songs. Those are the moments that I will remember most about this experience.

I sigh when I see a gigantic spray of roses on the kitchen counter. They're violet colored and immediately eye-catching. There's a note next to the flowers which says, "You looked beautiful tonight."

They're beautiful, but I can't smile. Gentry always used to buy me violet colored roses. It was something he did for every occasion and after every time he hurt me so bad that I blacked out. I start to shiver, feeling like I want to throw up or run at the same time. There's no way that these are from

Gentry though. It's just a fluke. One of the guys thought they were pretty, or one of their assistants picked them out on their behalf. I mean the security team never leaves my side, and the bus is always locked up, right?

Gentry had been surprisingly silent. There had been no objections to my divorce petition and since I hadn't asked for anything and I had nothing in the way of worldly possessions that Gentry could possibly want, it was moving along quickly. A part of me couldn't help but think that everything had been too easy to this point after three years of having to battle with him every day. But maybe for once in my life I had lucked out.

Feeling creeped out despite my pep talk to myself, I exit the bus to go wait for the guys in one of their dressing rooms while they finish some interviews and a few more VIP meet and greets. Dan and Jake, two of my security team, are waiting right outside the bus as I exit. After carefully punching the button that locks up the bus, we walk back to the venue.

Jesse gives me a huge grin when he sees me even though it's just been five minutes since I left. "Everything okay?" he mouths over a fan's head. I nod and smile, not wanting to interrupt their flow.

"You know this isn't going to last forever," says the cold, British voice that I've come to dread from beside me.

"What are you talking about, Miranda?" I ask, too exhausted to want to get into a battle of wits with her tonight.

"You and I both know that they're going to get tired of you riding their coattails eventually," she says, flicking an imaginary piece of lint off her pristine pantsuit. "The public and the label like your boys a little bad, and with you in the picture they don't get that."

I look at her incredulously. "The label wants them to be partying every night, getting fucked up out of their minds, and sleeping with every woman available?" I ask angrily.

"That image does nothing but distract from the fact that they are one of the most talented bands on the planet."

She gives me a grin. "I could have a band in their place within a week and no one would even miss them," she says striding away on her four-inch heels. "I suggest that you think long and hard about how much you love those men or if you're selfish enough to destroy them."

It feels like there's a rock in the pit of my stomach as I watch her walk away. I look back over and see Jensen looking at me, a frown on his face showing he clearly saw Miranda talking to me. They've tried their best to keep her away from me since she obviously hates me, but they can't be with me every second.

I watch Jesse and Tanner sign autographs while Jensen gives an interview, Miranda's words heavy on my mind. She was wrong. She had to be. Their fans liked their music, not just their reputation. They were born to be the stars they are, nothing could change that. And besides, wasn't it all a little bit rock n roll that they were sharing me if and when the public found out? I watch as an attractive blonde who I had seen at a few other shows places her hand on Jesse's chest. He looks uncomfortable at her familiarity, but a part of me knew that she had been one of his hookups in the past. I want to go over there and rip her hand off his chest. Jesse is mine. He loves me. She has no chance. But unfortunately, the best I could do today was turn around and strike up a conversation with the security team so I didn't have to watch.

Five minutes later I felt an arm around me. "Baby, let's go back to the bus," says Jensen in my ear. I immediately melt into him, glad that I can get away and that I don't have to do it alone. Sneaking a look behind me I see that the blonde fan is still lurking around Jesse even though he has succeeded in getting her to stop touching him. Yep, I need to go back to the bus before I went over there.

"So the interviewer asked me about my love life. He said

that rumor was that the band were changed men," says Jensen as we walk.

"Oh," I try to say casually. "And what did you say?"

He stops me and gently pulls me into his body. "What did you want me to say?" he asks, dragging his lips down my neck to that place in between my neck and my shoulder that drives me crazy.

"That you're with someone that makes you deliriously happy and that you're crazy in love with." I try to say it as a joke, but I can't help but wish that the whole world could know that they are mine.

He pulls his head up so he's looking me in the eyes. His eyes are that warm, gentle green right now that I only see when he's happy and relaxed. I love that they look that way right now.

"Would you believe me if I said those exact words in the interview?" he says to me, getting so close to my lips that we breathe each other's breaths.

My eyes widen and my heart feels like it's going to explode with hope. "You didn't!" I tell him, thinking he has to be joking.

"I didn't give names since we're still trying to protect you from the public eye as much as possible, but that's what I said. I'm tired of hiding the fact that I'm happy for the first time in five years. I want everyone to know that I'm taken, that we're all taken. And that's never going to change." He swings me around and every worry about the flowers, about Miranda...they all disappear in the light I see in his eyes.

We walk into the bus and I stop as soon as I see that every surface is covered in pink and white peonies. They're my favorite flower, and definitely not in season right now. It's more flowers than I've ever seen in one place. I also notice that there's no sign of any violet roses.

"This is amazing," I tell him, turning around to jump into his arms. "Thanks for putting up with us. I know it's been a long few weeks. I promise we will spoil you and romance you more in the future," he says, leaning in for a long kiss that leaves me breathless.

Hopping off of him, I go and examine all the flowers, touching the petals softly. I also try and see if the violet roses are under any of the other flowers, but there's still no sign of them.

"Did you happen to order a bouquet of violet roses?" I ask in a choked voice. Jensen looks confused. "No," he says slowly. "Are those your favorite flowers now. Should we have?"

"No... But I could have sworn I saw them when I first came in. There was even a note that said that I looked beautiful tonight." I pause before continuing. "They were the kind of roses that Gentry always gave me after he beat me," I admit with a pained whisper. I had gone out of my way not to talk about my marriage to Gentry with the guys. I didn't want him tainting this new life of mine, and it seemed like any mention of Gentry was destined to do that.

"You think they were from Gentry?" Jensen says in a too calm voice, a voice that seemed like he was doing everything he could to control it.

I try to laugh. "I'm sure it was nothing. They were probably meant for Miranda or something and delivered to the wrong place."

"Ya, I'm sure that's it," he says, in that same casual voice that seems so wrong. "I'm going to see where our food is. Stay here."

He's gone before I can even answer. The beeping sounding off as he leaves telling me that he locked the bus behind him.

They know something they aren't telling me, and I hate it. But I guess we're all entitled to our secrets. Aren't I keeping a huge one from them? Something tells me that our new lease on a life together depends on us keeping a few things for ourselves.

I feel a chilling apprehension that I chide myself for, a fear I'll lose him, that I will lose all of them, or maybe more accurately that I've never had any of them.

It's fifteen minutes before he comes back, looking harried, and also empty handed. "They didn't have our food ready?" I ask, gesturing to his empty hands.

His face slides into the unreadable look that he's perfected over the course of his life so well. "Pack up a few things. We have a surprise for you," he says, not answering my question.

"We only have two days off, right?" I ask, feeling excited despite the strange circumstances surrounding this surprise.

"Yep, but besides the interview we have to do tomorrow, we're going to make the most of it," he says, walking towards me and slapping my butt. "Now hurry up, you've got five minutes."

I grin at him, feeling like a little girl on Christmas morning at the prospect of the next two days. I race to the back bedroom and stuff every outfit I see into a bag. It's nice to actually like my clothes again, and I want to pack extra stuff since I don't know what we're doing.

Five minutes later I've grabbed my toothbrush and makeup, and I'm ready to go.

Jensen's on the phone speaking softly when I come out. When he sees me, he abruptly ends the call, making me a little sick inside. Gentry did that a lot in the early part of our marriage when he was still pretending he was a dutiful husband after it became clear that I wasn't keen on spreading my legs to someone who was beating me.

I try to shake away the feeling. Jensen isn't Gentry. Jesse and Tanner aren't Gentry. I won't ever have to worry about that again. It's a chant I have to keep telling myself as all my insecurities rear their ugly head.

"Who was that?" I ask, trying to keep my voice nonchalant.

"It was just Jesse. He's ready for us," he says in a way that doesn't seem like he's lying.

I hate that my mistakes are making me now doubt the best thing I've ever had. If they didn't want me, I wouldn't be here.

He holds out his hand to me, and I hate how hard it is for me to take it.

There's a black Escalade waiting for us right outside the bus, and I smile at the reminder of our past. Jensen must be thinking the same thing because he squeezes my hand when he sees it. We're quiet as we drive to whatever secret destination we're going to. I can't help but gape at the sprawling city around me. Pictures of New York didn't prepare me for the sheer enormity of the city. There's so much to see and do. I wish that we had two months to explore instead of two days.

We finally pull up in front of what looks like a very fancy hotel. Jensen tells me that it's a Ritz Carlton. He gestures out the other window where I can see the start of what I'm very much hoping is Central Park. "Are we staying here?" I ask excitedly.

"We thought it would be good to get a break from the bus," Jensen says, smiling at the excitement that's leaking out of me. As I step into the lobby of the hotel, I can't help but gasp in amazement. Gentry had money, his parents oozed it. But the wealth of our little town in the south was very different from how money was displayed here and in the rockstar world.

The lobby oozes luxury, and I'm trying to not look like the fish out of water that I am as Jensen leads me directly to the elevators. I can hear whispers as we walk, I'm sure news spreading quickly of the rockstar that's in residence. We're both silent on the elevator. Jensen leads me to what I presume is our room. He opens it and steps back, gesturing for me to step inside.

My eyes are as wide as dinner plates as I take in the

opulent suite. There are floor to ceiling windows that I imme-diately walk to. I gasp in amazement at the view of what has to be Central Park and the city around it. It's incredible. Looking back at Jensen I see that he's watching me with an inscrutable look. "This is amazing," I tell him softly as he walks to stand behind me, gathering me in his arms with his chin resting on my head.

"We want to give you everything, baby," he says. And it's such a sweet sentiment coming from my gruff caveman that I turn around in his arms and give him a soft kiss.

"This is wonderful, but all I want is all of you," I tell him. "You know that right? None of this is what makes me want you."

He looks at me and his eyes get that warm and lazy look that I love so much. "You're the only woman in the world that wants me for me and not what I can give them."

I was pretty sure that Cassidy, or whatever her name was, was head over heels in love with Jensen in whatever form she could get him, but I decided not to mention that.

Jensen orders what seems like every item on the room service menu and as soon as the feast arrives, we dig in. I haven't seen the other guys, but Jensen says they will be here soon. They have some band business to attend to apparently. I wasn't sure what band business they needed to do at midnight, but it did seem like the guys got busier and busier with obligations as the tour went on.

After eating, we decide to watch movies in bed despite the fact that I feel like I could be rolled out of the hotel room from being so full of so many delicious things. I take a shower alone, which I wasn't expecting, but Jensen is waiting for me in bed when I get out eating some of the gourmet chocolate bar from a gift basket the hotel had left as a courtesy for the guys.

I must have a pouty look on my face because Jensen laughs, and I lose myself for a minute in the way his smile transforms his entire face. His green eyes crinkle at the edges and his full lips stretch to his cheeks. He's so fucking beautiful that I can't help but toss aside the towel I'm wearing and climb into his lap. His arms come around me, anchoring me to his body.

"Kiss me," I demand, straddling him. He looks up at me and smiles, that secret smile of his that I love so much. He lifts up a piece of chocolate and motions for me to open my lips. I do and he pops a piece in. I chew it slowly, wondering what he was doing. The second after I swallow his lips are on mine.

He kisses me slowly at first, not budging my lips open at all. His hands are around my back, his fingertips running over my skin. and I tremble slightly in his arms. He opens my lips with his own, and I fall under the magic that is Jensen's mouth. His teeth nip my lips and I sigh into the kiss, my heart beating erratically in my chest. Jensen pulls back and slides his hands up to cup my jaw.

"Ari." I open my eyes slowly.

"Jensen," I say back. His eyes trace my face, and his hands push my hair away. "My everything."

I start to ask him what he means, but he pulls me to him again and kisses me until I have to pull away to catch my breath. I lay my head on his shoulder and close my eyes. His arms tighten around me. Safe. That was the word that I thought whenever I was in Jensen's arms. I knew I should strive to be a more independent woman, I knew that. But it was nice to have someone so dedicated to myself and my happiness for once in my life. Or three someones…

I press a kiss to his neck, reveling in this feeling of contentment. Outside of the bubble that was us, my mind was in a hundred places. Frustrated with feeling like I'm not contributing to anything and feeling like a prisoner from all the safety precautions. But being in Jensen's arms wasn't a prison. It was a home.

"When all of this is over, where do you want to go?" he asks.

I think about his question for a minute. "Paris."

"Then we'll go."

That was it – that was Jensen, always making sure things happened that I wanted. I knew I wouldn't go to Paris without Jensen, nor would he go without me. And while that was comforting, a blanket of contentment, I still felt a tug. I couldn't name the emotion that tugged me, but it was there. A nagging in the back of my mind. Reminding me that things could change in an instant.

ARIANA

I t was 1:00pm and daylight was wasting. Jensen had woken me up at 6:00am saying that the guys had inter-views with a few radio stations this morning, but as soon as they got back, we would go out. That was seven hours ago, and I had just gotten a text that Miranda had booked a few more surprise things for them and it was going to be later than they thought by the time they got back.

Despite the lavishness of the suite, it felt like a prison. I was desperate to get out, to explore the city. Despite all the places we had been so far up and down the eastern seaboard, we were never in one place for long enough to actually see anything. I knew I shouldn't complain, after all I could be scheduled for lunch at the country club or getting beat by Gentry, but I still found myself wanting more.

I decide to go for a run. I need to run—run from the chaos in my head, run from the guys and the complications of not only their life, but the challenges knotted so indelibly into my own. I need to feel the freedom that only running can bring me.

Gentry's psychotic need for me looking as good as

possible had led to me taking up running. I was never comfortable doing tennis with the other wives or going to the gym where it felt like there were eyes on me all the time, but I did enjoy running.

With the guy's obsession with security following my every move, and me not wanting to lug five humongous men behind me on a run, I hadn't gone running once. That was going to change now.

I bite away the thought of the roses from the day before. I hadn't heard from Gentry, there was no reason to think that he would be here in New York City following me around. Slipping on my sports bra, hoodie, leggings, and Nikes, I opened the door to the hallway and look out, expecting to see my usual team.

There is no one there. A small chill runs down my spine, but I'm so desperate to get out and explore that I ignore it. I slip to the elevator expecting one of the security team to call my name out at any time. There's no one in the lobby either as I walk through it, and a few more steps and I'm out in the city.

It's a gorgeous, crisp, perfect day, and I'm immediately entranced by the sights, smells, and people that I see. I decide to run through some of Central Park since it's daylight and there's a million people around to keep it safe.

My muscles strain at first from my efforts, but eventually I find myself in that zone that I've always loved. I pass children walking with their parents, other runners, and bloggers taking pictures by a bridge. There's food stands set up, and I take a small break to scarf down a hotdog from one of the stands. It seemed like a very New York thing to do.

There are a herd of bicyclists coming towards me at one point, so I turn left down a less crowded path. After I've run a mile, I realize that there's not very many people around this area and the trees are denser. I find myself running faster until the path spits me out and I find myself back on the bustling city sidewalk, the Park behind me.

I keep going, farther and farther until I have no idea where I am or where I'm going.

A shiver runs down my spine, even though I'm sweating. The sun hovers above the city skyline. Tall brown and gray buildings of varying heights line the streets. For blocks I run and free my mind, concentrating on the wind at my back, the tempo of my breath, and the pull of long-dormant muscles in my legs. It's not long before the city becomes a blur and my thoughts stray to the guys, and how I fit into the intricate web of their life. I thought that our love could simplify the craziness of their life, but there's no slowing down the most popular band in the world. Am I strong enough to endure the demands of their career? Will I forever be detached from the three of them in public? How is it we can work? They always act like they don't have a single doubt that it will all work out, that we'll find a way, but doubts to the validity of that statement, mainly from Miranda, are becoming harder to ignore.

How is a happy ending possible when the disparity between us is so great? I still have some secrets, ones that I want to take with me to the grave if possible. And I'm sure they do too. Everything seems so overwhelming.

And then I laugh, a bubble bursting from my chest with such freedom I stop in my tracks. I'm so overreacting. Leaning against a stop sign at a cross-section, I smile through my panted breath. I love them, more than I ever thought I was capable of loving anything or anyone. Their career isn't going anywhere and worrying constantly about my place in it won't strengthen our relationship.

I just need to find myself so that I can fit in with their life and not feel like such an interloper. I know it's possible. Cutting across the street, I head in what I think is the direction of the hotel. Footsteps fall in line with mine; it must be another runner coming up behind me.

For the fun of it, I pick up my pace to make the runner work for it before he or she catches me. My breath spikes as I push myself faster, expecting for the person to pass me at any moment. I run into a side street without stopping for the possibility of traffic. Silence. There's no one there. Glancing behind me doesn't produce anything but the dingy brick of the building I just rounded. Footsteps echo in the narrow alley I use as a shortcut—first mine and then a second set. Driving harder, I propel myself the final few blocks to the hotel.

Shop doors blur as I streak by. Panic bursts in my already burning chest as I chance a look behind me. The shadow of a figure turns the corner. Lines are elongated into a grotesquely misshapen man by sun stretching across the buildings. I dart into the road. A horn blares, the car it belongs to screeches to a stop inches from my frozen form. Shit.

Waving a lame apology, I race into the hotel twenty feet away. Hands on my knees, I gulp in air. Through the window, I find a quiet street; no one is walking or running in my wake. But I didn't imagine it. The heavy tread of falling feet still echoes in my ears. With one last look out the door I turn to the elevators and where hopefully the guys are waiting for me.

I t's not exactly the peaceful homecoming I was hoping for. Jensen is pacing the front room of the suite with his phone pressed to his ear. "Dan, this shit better not happen again." His hard, almost frantic eyes find mine. "No excuses. I've been clear about my expectations, let me state them again—every minute, every day, your entire team, no exceptions." His chest rises and falls as if he went for a jog, but that's not the case because he's in a very tight pair of boxer briefs and nothing else.

Something happened.

"No, I haven't. Yes, I fucking understand you think you got a text from us, but that obviously wasn't the case. We have people looking into how that happened as we speak. No matter what you think you get from us, unless you hear one of us say it out loud, you stay with her." After a pause, Jensen says, "Don't ever let this happen again."

His eyes never leave mine as he ends the call and tosses his cell on the couch. I grab a water from the fridge and drink it down while watching his gaze streak over my sweaty body.

"I went for a run when your meetings got extended." I admit the obvious.

"So I see," he says in a strained voice. He picks up the phone again and presses the phone to his ear. "She's back." He pauses as he listens to someone who I think is Jesse yelling over the line. "She decided to go for a run." He listens again. "Just get back here." He tosses the phone down again angrily.

"I thought maybe I'd be back before you guys returned," I say, not sure why I'm even bothering to defend myself when I did nothing wrong.

"You should have texted us. One of us, or your security team could have gone with you when we returned," he growls and steps toward me. He's angry and I can't tell if he's upset with me, or the something that happened.

"Are you mad at me?" I ask incredulously.

"Why would I be, Ariana?" His voice is calm, yet I know he's not since he used my full name.

"You think I'm angry because you left alone," he pauses for a shaking breath, "in a strange city, without telling anyone where you were going, or how long you would be...."

I realize that I am the something that has happened.

"That's not true, I had my phone with me."

"Did you bother to use it. Is it even on? Did you not think for a fucking second to at least send us a text?" His tone rises and his eyes flash a green I've never seen before. His anger is a cold, dark, menacing thing and it reminds me of those first couple of days when he acted like he couldn't stand the sight of me.

I pull my cell phone out of my sports bra and cringe when I see that it is indeed off. I had forgotten to charge it the night before and apparently it had died on my run. The look on my face confirms his accusations.

"I can't find you in a city with millions of people if your damn cell phone isn't on. A turned off cell phone doesn't tell me what fucking direction you went in, how long ago you left, what path you were on! Did you even stop to contemplate the crime rate in this city, the number of—" He stops and shudders.

"No, I didn't," I say weakly, remembering the footsteps following behind me at the end of my run. "I'm sorry. I was around tons of people in a public place. I didn't think you would worry about me if I was just gone for a bit."

His brow digs into three deep, angry lines. He moves so close I have to tilt my head back to hold eye contact. "Not worry?" The words fall from his tongue as if they're poison. "Not worry?" he says again. "All we fucking do is worry about you, Ariana. Tanner and Jesse are out combing the city for you right now risking the likelihood that they are going to be mobbed by fans. I've been on the phone since we got back trying all of our contacts. Do you not know how much we need you? How much I need you?"

Comprehension barely sinks in before his mouth crushes mine. Melting into him, I dig my fingers into his hair and stay flush against his hard body. He holds my face with both hands so I can't step away from the frustration he takes out on me with lashes of his tongue. I match his need, the danger of my apparently thoughtless run rolling off me in waves. He takes it, takes me until I can't breathe but he doesn't let me go, punishing my lips with his for the careless worry I caused. He rips away, panting. "Damn it, Ariana—don't ever fucking do that again." His mouth finds mine, this time in a tempered but passionate kiss that frankly has me breathing harder than the miles I've just run.

I cling to him, arms around his neck as he maneuvers us to the bathroom, turning the shower on hot before he strips me. My hoodie is first, up and over my head; my bra follows it to the floor. He drops to his knees, eyes on mine as he licks below my navel and removes my shoes one at a time. I'm on to his game as he pulls my pants to the floor, so slow I'm panting with need by the time he's done.

He kisses up my leg, runs his nose along the lace of my underwear as he breathes me in. I grab his hair and moan at the movement. I spread my legs. Slowly, so damn slow, he peels my underwear off and the warm air tickles my skin. I whimper when his breath fans over me.

"Please," I beg.

He stands.

Um, excuse me? I want to scream, back to your knees, but then his boxer briefs are off and I sigh with relief because he steps into me. I hiss as my bare chest meets his chest. My arms are around his neck and I lift to find his mouth, but he turns his head and navigates us into the streaming water. Shampoo is first. Every tender stroke dissolves his anger and fear and works me into a bigger ball of need. It's delicious, but so is what's jutting into my stomach. I reach for him and he's quick to knock my hand away. I groan and he smiles, tipping my head into the water to rinse and then repeat with conditioner.

My body is next. He soaps up every available inch. Collarbone and arms; my breasts he takes on one at a time, tugging on the tips. I gasp and arch into him. But he moves to my back and butt, around to my stomach and then, achingly slowly, he moves between my legs. Parting me with his fingers, he rubs. I drop my forehead to his chest, rolling my hips with the rhythm of his hand. I'm so close.

"Jensen," I breathe into his neck. My nails sink into his shoulder as he does it again. He stops and drops to his knees. Yes, I love his mouth. I fist his hair, but he washes my feet.

No!

"Your little run left us little time for anything but to dress and leave before our reservations this evening." He smiles— the bastard smiles.

"That's not fair."

I jerk away from him as he stands, and I slip my hand between my thighs. If he won't do it, I'll make him watch as I do. His nostrils flare and he's on me in a second. In the next my arms are above my head and I'm cold, pressed against the tile.

"Don't you dare," he snarls. "You made a choice, suffer with it until one of us has time to work the pleasure out of you. It's ours."

"I didn't know it was dangerous," I hiss.

"And now you do," he replies.

He wants to be mad, fine. Rage simmers beneath my skin and out of my mouth one word at a time. "Let go of me."

Understanding flickers in his eyes. He's pushed me too far. As soon as his grip loosens, I fly from the shower and on my way out of the room I grab two towels. One I wrap around my aching and heavy breasts. Damn that man. I don't know how to do angry with Jensen.

Everything's new for us: I mean we're for all intents and purposes living together when we haven't seen each other for five years. Everything about our relationship is on warp speed. At times that speed is too much.

I take it out on my hair, scrubbing it with a towel until it's sticking up all over the place. When he appears in the door-way, naked as a jaybird, I turn away. My movements are staccato and when he sighs my name, I start the hair drier and hum "Girl in the White Dress" because it's stuck in my head from the concert last night. It infuriates me more. Everything I do is out of spite. My hair in a high ponytail to bare my neck, the smallest thong I own slips into place. The tightest dress the stylist gave me follows it and note to self: add extra sway to my ass at every possible moment. I add dramatic makeup as my final fuck-you. I look good. Slipping into four-inch heels, I add that hip-sway and saunter into the suite. For a second, I feel like a little girl playing dress-up of something that she's not, but I push through and pretend I'm all that.

He's on the phone by the window, a replay of when I came home from my run. I bypass his eyes, yet notice that he's wearing the white shirt I like that shows off his deep tan. It may be his surrender flag, but too bad. Battle on. I do good mad and I'm ferocious. I turn away to throw some things into my black clutch.

The flush of energy is my first clue he's behind me and then the heat radiating from his chest confirms it. His hand lands on my hip, as if to turn me toward him, but I stiffen and stand my ground.

"This is how it's going to be?" he asks. Anger burns below my skin and I almost scream it out of me and at him.

"This is how you decided it needed to be." I swallow and turn. His eyes show how he hurts, but he crossed a line with me just then. He needs to know and understand the consequences that follow a stunt like his in the shower. I hear the door open and close and I know that Jesse and Tanner have just arrived.

"Jensen, I'm sure you can figure out that when you're in an abusive relationship like I have been in for the past three years, there's a lot of "withholding" that occurs. I will not let that happen in this relationship."

Shame crosses his features and he takes a step towards me. I hold up my hand. "Don't do it again," I tell him, my voice shaking as I try to hold in the tears. Turning I look at Jesse and Tanner who are both standing there, obviously relieved to see me, but obviously unsure of what to say at the moment after what they just walked in on.

"Shall we go?" I say in a false, bright voice that makes everyone in the room cringe. Jesse nods and holds out his hand. And away we go...

We end up going to see Wicked on Broadway after a delicious dinner at a restaurant that had people waiting in a line around the corner to try and get in. It should have been amazing, but the fight after my run stayed with me, dampening everything else. We were all quiet in the elevator riding up to our suite, and when we arrived at the suite, I immediately head to one of the spare bedrooms where I've been storing my stuff for some alone time. I wouldn't be sleeping with any of them tonight.

Pulling open the doors to the bedroom, I expect the giant bed I spied in here yesterday, but I don't expect the giant red wrapped package sitting in the middle of the bed....

The gorgeous golden and white room fades around me as my attention focuses on the package. Somehow there's something inside of me that tells me that it's not from one of the guys. Even knowing that I'm being stupid, I open the top of the package with trembling hands. Inside there are black and white photographs and papers with type-written words.

I pick up one of the pieces of paper. My hands shake as I realize what I'm looking at. It's a hospital record. My hospital record. Of a night and the weeks afterwards that I have done everything I can to forget. I'm rooted to the spot, the paper dangling in my hand. Unable to step away—unable to speak, just staring. The photographs are of me, some with the guys, but others just of me. I recognize some of them from my time with Gentry, pictures of me sleeping or the black and blue on my body after Gentry hit me, but there's also pictures since the tour. Ones of me in the audience watching the guys, of me singing on stage, of me singing during soundcheck. It's a timeline of my time with the guys so far. There's picture after picture, ending with me walking into the hotel last night with Jensen.

The piece de résistance waits for me at the bottom of the box. It's a shot of me that the police must have taken that night so long ago. I'm in my hospital bed, exposed and broken. There's a message scrawled in red below the picture. "Found you," it says.

I look away quickly noticing that all of my beautiful new clothes have been torn off my hangers and are laying ripped into pieces on the floor. They're drenched in a bloody red paint and there's a dried white substance intermixed with the red paint. Bile rises, my hand flying up to my mouth to hold it in at the sight of a solitary violet flower placed on the pillow where my head would lie. Fear takes over and my heart races. I step backwards until I'm standing in the entry of the room, my eyes glued on the box.

When my knees give out, I grab the doorframe to catch myself, and choke on a cry. The weight pressing in on my chest is suffocating as my eyes dart back to that picture. A picture that I didn't even know existed.

Short, jagged breaths are lodged in my throat. Help, I think, but it doesn't seem like any words come out.

"Princess? What's wrong?" Tanner is a small hint of sound, barely recognizable while I'm in my faraway space. I try to respond, I do, but words won't form. The best I can offer is a mournful whimper, which sounds dejected as it echoes against the walls. He walks past me and confusedly looks at the contents of the box. Another pair of hands reach me before Tanner's harsh and much louder expletive of "Holy fuck" sounds across the room.

I'm wrapped tight into what I know is Jesse's chest. I suspect we're moving, but I don't actually feel anything. I'm no longer present in any way. I feel nothing. I can make as if it never happened. That night never happened. Everything is okay. I tuck away everything nice and neat in a pile I won't unfold until I'm forced to.

J   **esse**
"Bathroom and a shower," she murmurs, hoarse from the screaming that I don't think she even realized was happening. "Please." Her fingers sink into my arm.

"Anything you want. Wrap your arms around my neck." She weighs a fraction of what I think she should. She was thin when she came to us, and the weeks since then haven't changed that. We haven't done our jobs good enough of making her happy. I squeeze as much as I dare given how fragile she suddenly seems to me.

We're in the hotel's largest suite, courtesy of the public relations nightmare it would be for the hotel if the media got ahold of this story and how someone apparently was able to impersonate a maid and gain access to our suite while we were out.

Fucking hell. Gentry was going to pay for this. There were no good shots of him breaking into the suite; he'd been too smart not to come disguised, but we knew it was him. He had been stalking Ari for weeks and we had been keeping it from her. Intercepting the packages and the notes, keeping a security team on her 24/7. Despite all of that he had managed somehow to get on our bus with its top of the line security system to deliver flowers, and then later get into our room. He had somehow managed to reroute his phone so it looked like our security team was getting texts from us telling them to take a break and give Ari space.

I can't help but squeeze her tighter thinking of the danger she was in during her run today. I breathe in her scent as I half-laugh and half-cry in exhaustion, I've lived and died what feels like a million times today worrying about her. I've been in meetings with execs at the record label and with the security company trying to come up with a plan to keep her safe. Of course, they wanted her to leave the tour, but we wouldn't let that happen.

Once we're in one of the suite's lavish marble bathrooms, I softly brush a kiss against her lips, relishing the feeling of her fingers responding and teasing my nape. She's my life. She's all of our lives.

"I wish I could go back and take this away from you," I whisper into her hair thinking of that picture of her lying in the hospital bed. A picture I know nothing about but know that it represents an unspeakable horror for her. Possibly the key to why she did what she did all those years ago.

She sniffles and nods, but when she opens her mouth a cry comes, and then another. I take her nape and tuck her into my shoulder, my lips to her hair. I'm in no hurry. Words will come when she's ready, and I'll be here to listen. For now, I'll live in the sweet sound of her silence.

I haven't a clue on how to make this better, so I do the only thing I can—hold her. Through my hands stroking her back and my breath in her hair my lips murmuring into her forehead, I try to show her how adored she is, as precious as the rarest gem. How I thank God with every heartbeat she is mine.

I take in her contented sigh, but know I have to let her down when she starts to squirm. "Easy now." I set her feet on the tiles, but keep my hands hovering around her waist as she stands, eyes closed to the glare of the lights. It's a good thing I do when she nearly crumbles. She presses her nose to my neck through the minute it takes to get her settled on the toilet and then I start the shower so it can heat up before she gets in.

"I'll give you a minute of privacy while I go get some clothes for you. Don't move."

I hold in my grimace. She's so fragile, sitting with her arms wrapped around her body, her eyes wild amidst the ebony hair that's framing her unusually pale face.

"I'll be right back, okay?"

"Ya," she murmurs, but I can see her trembling lips. My beautiful girl is holding on by a thread. I close the door on her feelings only to be confronted by Jensen's and Tanner's. Tanner is talking to a detective in the New York City police department on the phone. Jensen is sitting on the couch looking through the contents of the box. He shouldn't have moved the box just in case there were fingerprints, but I don't have it in me to say anything. I know that the last thing Ari wants is for anyone to see the contents of that box.

I grab a pair of sweats and a shirt from my closet knowing that Ari finds comfort in wearing our things. It's also out of necessity though since that bastard destroyed all the new clothes Ari was so proud of. I'm about to go back in, but I can hear Ari sobbing inside. I lean my forehead against the cool wood of the doorway, listening to her sob and letting her have a moment. Time is suspended as it goes on. Guilt steals my breath as I wrestle with the fact that we all just gave up on her five years ago. We should have known that Ari wouldn't have changed her mind, especially that quickly. We should have been less interested in our own broken hearts, and more concerned about hers.

I hate myself and the decisions I made. It brought us here, listening to an ocean of her tears. I crack open the door an inch. It's enough room for me to see through the steam and into the mirror reflecting Ariana as she steps into the shower. I softly close the door and let her shower even as the sight of all her skin makes me ache to join her even in this situation.

I hear a crash in the living room, and I make my way there to see Tanner and Jensen looking like they're about to exchange blows.

"What the fuck is going on? You two can't control your

testosterone even in a situation like this?" I bark at them angrily. Tanner takes the opportunity to rip the papers out of Jensen's hands that I hadn't noticed he was holding.

"Asshole here was about to start reading through her medical records," he says, going over to the giant fireplace against the wall and throwing the papers in. He stands there until they're completely burned to ashes.

"Don't you want to know?" asks Jensen in a frustrated voice, pulling at his hair so it sticks up all over the place.

"It's not our business," snaps Tanner. "She'll tell us when she's ready. I don't see her asking us about everything that's happened over the last five years."

Jensen flinches. I don't think any of us want that. The three of us have had our share of events we want to forget, and would rather Ari never hear about.

I hear the shower turn off, and I turn to leave. "Get all of that burned," I tell them, making the executive decision that no one else is going to see those documents. "And try not to kill each other," I add sarcastically as I leave the room.

Ari's toweling off as I enter the room. She still looks pale, but she looks slightly better than she did before her shower. I look away when she drops the towel and starts to pull on my sweats. She walks over to me when she finishes getting dressed.

"I ordered your favorite dinner," I tell her as we walk into the bedroom she's chosen. She tries for a smile, a slight bend to her lip when I pull the lid back to show a perfectly cooked ribeye that I actually ordered from one of the nicest steak-houses in New York and her favorite sides of mashed potato and creamed spinach. It's her favorite, but Ari picks at the steak to eat more like a bird than a woman who has barely eaten today since she didn't even pretend to eat at dinner, and I know that she skipped lunch after the fight with Jensen. Sleep is what she wants and I brush a kiss across Ari's fore-head and whisper, "I'll be back, I won't leave." I'll never leave her but she's already asleep before she can hear my reassurance.

After I've checked that Jensen and Tanner haven't killed each other and that all the documents and pictures have been burned, I go in and lie next to Ari. Relief washes through me when she rolls into my chest as if she's as desperate for me, as I am for her touch and sweet scent. But rest is out of reach. I lie awake petrified about how I'm going to keep this perfect angel safe.

It seems like minutes later that I'm blinking awake as my cell phone starts to ring. I struggle to get my bearings since I'm thinking that I've only been asleep for a minute.

"Good morning," Ariana says, as if she's been awake for hours.

By her appearance, maybe she has. She has a new outfit on that consists of a sleek black pencil dress and four-inch heels that have her legs seeming limitless. No sign of the trauma from the night before-only gorgeous Ari. Her hair is pulled harshly back away from her face and she's wearing a soft pink lipstick. She looks more like a politician's wife than she does the girlfriend of a rockstar. She's still beautiful to distraction though, and I find myself obsessing over getting a chance to kiss those pink lips. She bites the bottom one, sucking it into her mouth.

"Something wrong?" she asks.

"No." I shake my head. "It's just a different look than usual. Did the stylist bring over more clothes?"

"I ordered it from downstairs actually. Did you know you can order clothes just like you can room service?" she says in awe as she checks her appearance in a small mirror hanging on the wall above a dresser.

"Ari?" I call for her attention because she's so different from the terrified and fragile girl from last night. She's actually acting different from how I've ever seen her. She wraps a dainty necklace around her neck that I recognize as one that Jensen bought for her and works to clasp it.

"Hm?" Her gaze follows me as I stand and walk to her side.

"Are you alright? Why are you up? I was kind of expecting to stay in bed all day after yesterday."

"Miranda has you booked solid today and then we have to leave this afternoon for the show in Boston. I didn't want to wake you until the last minute because I knew you probably didn't sleep very much last night. You should shower. We have about an hour before you have to leave." She turns and brushes her lips against my cheek.

"We can take the day off," I say to her reflection, because I can't move. What the hell is going on here? Blinking doesn't bring on reality; I'm stuck in an alternate universe. I've woken up to a Ari from a different planet, one who wears dresses that belong more in church than in the life that we're creating together. "Ari," I say again.

She turns to me and for a second, I can see past the mask she's wearing, and what I see takes my breath away. Anger so hot and foreboding that I'm scared we'll never be able to get past it. "You should have told me," she whispers looking away from me. "You all should have told me." She grips the side of the doorway. "You'd better get ready. I'll order breakfast."

Our eyes meet again before she leaves and for a brief second, she cracks. Chin trembling, tears misting, until she blinks them away and turns, unwilling to look at me.

"Go get ready," she whispers. "I just need some time."

"What does that mean?"

"It means I don't want to talk about it. Not yet."

I could push her, something we've done before, but I have a feeling that whatever happened in that picture that shows a scared young girl on an examination table, it could destroy us all. I grab my hair, torn. This is my torture. "Tell me what to do. I want to be whatever you need to get through this, but I'm not sure what that is."

Looking up, those spectacular golden eyes blinking away the mist, she says on a faint whisper, "Wait for me." The knife living in my gut twists, and I nod.

"Promise you'll talk to us when you're ready. Even if it's in anger, promise me."

"One day, I will."

She leaves the room without another glance back.

12
THEN

ARIANA

Kryptonite. That's what those boys are to me I think as I stand outside my trailer preparing to go inside after another of the band's concerts. It's late but I still feel wired thinking about the new songs they introduced tonight. They made me itch to grab the notebook that I have hidden in my room and start writing more of my own songs.

The front door suddenly swings open. "What are you doing standing out there?" sneers David in a slurred voice. I avoid these kinds of interactions at all costs and I'm like a deer in the headlights for a moment as I stare at him. His eyes are bright red, and the room is smoky behind him. All I hope is that they aren't doing something like cooking meth. That's all I need is for the trailer to blow up and blow me up along with it while I'm sleeping innocently in my bed.

"Get in here," he says, grabbing my arm so hard that I know there's going to be a bruise there in the morning. I look around for my mother, hoping she's still awake. She's nowhere to be found. Number one on my list of how to survive is to never find myself alone with David and that's exactly where I'm finding myself now.

I try to wrench my arm out of his grip. The move catches him off guard and before he can grab me again, I'm out the door. It had been a minute since I'd had to do this, and my heart beats a thousand beats a minute as I sprint through the unkempt grass to who knows where. I would call Jensen, but he's been going through so much since his mom died that I don't want to bother him. And the other guys already do enough for me as it is. Maybe Amberlie could pick me up.

I get to the road and I'm pulling out my cell phone to call her when I notice a familiar black Escalade parked in the same place where I left it. I never let the guys drop me off by my trailer because I don't want David to ever see the guys' nice vehicles and start to try and get things from them.

Walking up to the passenger window, I see Jensen slouched down, playing a game on his phone. I tap on the window and he jumps, hitting his head on the window. I hide my smile and open the door after he recovers and opens it up.

"You scared the crap out of me," he says, rubbing his head embarrassedly. He suddenly realizes that it's strange for me to have come out to the road at 1:00 in the morning when he just dropped me off. Just as strange as him still hanging around where he dropped me off...

"Why are you still here?" I ask before he can start any of the questions I'm sure that he has.

"Just didn't feel like going home," he mutters dejectedly, saying something that's no surprise. Since his mom passed, he's been a little lost. He was still in his apartment with Tanner and Jesse and although they did everything they could to be supportive, there were just some things that you couldn't understand unless you had been through it.

"Why are you out here?" he asks before I can say something else to distract him.

I sigh, trying to think of what to say. I've never let on how truly bad it is for me at home. We're already coming from completely different social backgrounds, I don't need them to feel sorry or try to do something if they found out about Terry and David's drug habits.

"Just some family stuff," I finally say. I know that Jensen wants to ask more questions, but he holds his tongue. We sit in the car in silence, Lana Del Ray's Young and Beautiful playing softly in the background. It makes me think about all the things I don't like to think about, like what if the guys don't suddenly think I'm so great if they make it big. What will happen when there's far more beautiful girls to grab their attention. Will they still want me? Will I still hold a place in their hearts?

"Let's go for a drive," Jensen says, and he takes off before I can say anything. Settling into my seat I pull my seatbelt on. I watch the shadows that you can only see at night as we pass through town and out to the road that drives by the river.

"I just can't stop thinking about how I could have saved her," he says in a gravelly voice. It comes out like he hadn't meant to say anything, but it had just popped out of his mouth.

"Your sister?" I ask. He shakes his head. "My mom. I know I should have saved my sister. I can't seem to save anyone I'm supposed to." He looks at me. "You won't even let me try and help you. Why are you even here? Do you just feel sorry for me?" he spits out in a hurt voice.

My eyes widen. Why am I here? Do I just feel sorry for him?

Has Jensen forgotten who he is? Who I am?

"You don't believe that, do you?" I immediately say. He doesn't say anything. He just pulls the car over at an overlook that looks out over the river.

I get on my knees in the seat and take his hand in both of mine. He's covering his face with his other hand and I know that if he took his hand away there would be tears in his eyes.

"Oh, Jensen," I sigh. "You and Tanner and Jesse have done everything to take care of me." I take a deep breath feeling myself start to tear up. It's an unfortunate habit I have that I usually end up crying whenever anyone else is sad.

He groans when he hears the hitch in my voice, dropping his hand from his face and leaning over to me to lick a tear from my face before it can fall to our lap. His heavy breath fans over my mouth as he does so. I try to force away the shiver tickling my spine, to hide how he affects me since this feels hardly like the time for lust. But I can't.

I belong to him and I want him to belong to me. More than anything I want to find my place next to this man, next to Tanner and Jesse. Jensen lightly strokes the skin peeking out from the top of my shirt and I shiver and give off a desperate sound that I've never heard come out of my mouth before.

He responds by practically growling, it's a low vibration that warms the depth of his eyes. Leaning in to murmur against my mouth, he says, "Let me inside, Ari." My gosh. This man with his scorching good looks, his smooth tongue, and wicked hands is no match for me.

"Let me in," he demands again, and yet the simple statement is laced with desperation and need. But it's his eyes that grab hold of mine and won't let go. Pleading. My hands find their way to his neck, circling to hold him in place and feel his pulse under my thumb. Life.

"Jensen, it's all going to be okay," I whisper, knowing that we're both letting our lust prevent us from saying all the other things we should be talking about in this moment laced with all the pain of our broken lives. My heart can't help but thunder in my chest as he brushes a kiss against my lips. It can't help but explode when he groans my name.

"It doesn't make sense that an angel like you would want someone like me," he says in a pained voice as he strokes his tongue in my mouth once again as he devours my mouth.

I pull away. "Who wants a love that makes sense anyway?" I whisper back. I'm rewarded with a smile that seems to light up the whole night sky as it streams in through the moonroof that's open above us.

We don't say anything else that we should for the rest of the night. We let our hands and lips do the talking even if we never cross that line that I desperately want. By the time the sun hits the horizon, I've forgotten the reason why I'd ended up in Jensen's car that night in the first place.

ARIANA

I'm always on the lookout for Gentry. I imagine that I see him in every crowd, that he's hiding in every shadow. I feel like a fraction of myself, more like the scared, abused wife than the woman I thought I was becoming. That's the thing about fear, it comes at you when you least expect it and all you can do is try to get through it to the other side.

Tanner comes up beside me on the bus. I bring my hand to his hair, and push it away from his forehead. "Tanner with longer hair is my favorite," I say, dragging my nails down the side of his scalp. His other hand grabs my wandering one and he pulls it to his lips, placing the softest kiss on my knuckles.

"What are you thinking about?" he asks as he sits down and pulls out the control system so we can pick a movie.

"Just wondering what he's planning next," I reluctantly admit. The guys have probably gotten sick of the fact that I seem to live in my daydreams now a days.

Tanner brushes a kiss along my hairline. "When…" he trails away, his eyes glued to something outside the window. "Fuck."

"What?" I ask, afraid to turn around.

"It's Miranda," he says through gritted teeth. She seems to be hovering around even more the last few stops. After Boston we had gone to Cleveland and Lansing and now, we were in the parking lot of the stadium in Indianapolis where the Colts play. It had been a lot of driving over the last few days with not a lot of rest in between. Maybe I should have been resting, but when I was keeping an eye out for Gentry, that wasn't really very possible.

Tanner runs a hand through his hair to try and tame it. He tucks my hair behind my ears and kisses me softly, probably not even realizing what he was doing since taking care of me seemed to be second nature to all of them.

The hunger that had been missing over the past week all of a sudden roars back to life and my hands reach to clutch him to me. Tanner loosens my grip and shakes his head apologetically.

"Hellooo," she calls out in a breezy voice that I'm not accustomed to. My eyes flash to the door of the bus which has just opened to let Miranda in. A second later she appears, looking immaculate as always in sky high heels and a tight pencil skirt. Her eyes light up when she sees Tanner, giving me an uncomfortable feeling as that look has started to appear more frequently. And despite her attractiveness, she was at least twenty years older than him. And he wasn't into cougars. I could attest to that.

"Ariana, so glad you're here," she coos, and Tanner and I both look at her as if she's out of her mind. The last thing Miranda usually thinks is that she's glad that I'm here.

"The opening act for tonight had to pull out due to their lead singer's illness and the label thought it would be wonderful if Ariana were to fill in for them tonight." She claps her hands giddily as if she's an excited teenager presented with her first car.

Despite the fact that it's Miranda presenting the idea, a thrill of excitement rises up inside of me at the thought of performing on stage again. I hadn't sung in front of anyone but the guys since that first performance since they thought that bringing me on stage again would be too much of a risk with Gentry following me. Of course, I hadn't known that Gentry was following me. So, for the past month it had just felt like they had thought I did terrible since they didn't want a repeat performance.

I open my mouth to respond, but Jensen storms into the lounge area. "Absolutely not," he snaps. "We haven't heard from Gentry since the hotel incident and we have no idea where he is. It's not safe."

My heart sinks even though I know he's right. Miranda looks like Jensen just killed her cat. Which is strange since I've never gotten the impression that Miranda thinks I'm particularly talented.

"It would be an excellent opportunity for Ari to start making a name for herself," she says and I'm even more suspicious by her use of my nickname.

"I'd better not," I finally say, even though the decision has already been made for me.

I try not to resent the increased overbearing nature of my three guys, but it's hard not to. All I want is to feel like an equal partner in my relationship with them. But that's hard to do when they're making all the decisions for my life, often without informing me of their decisions until after the fact.

Miranda leaves in a huff muttering about what a waste of space I am, as if it's my fault that I can't perform tonight.

Tanner turns the movie back on that we had been watching before Miranda arrived, and Jensen leaves the room to finish working out.

As I sit next to Tanner, in the same bus as all of the guys, I realize that somehow, I've become incredibly lonely. This wasn't what I pictured when I thought about what it would be like to tour the world together.

This can't continue.

The guys are doing sound check while I sit on a couch in the greenroom, surrounded by security. I didn't feel like watching them even though I usually never miss a chance to watch them sing, soundcheck or not.

"Ariana," says a voice. I look up and see Clark, the band's agent. He hasn't been with us for most of the tour since he has a roster of other superstar clients he has to keep in line along with the band.

"How have you been?" he asks, sitting next to me.

"Fine," I reply with a tight smile, unable to muster the proper enthusiasm I'm sure a rockstar's girlfriend is supposed to have.

"I haven't heard that you've performed recently?" he asks.

"It just hasn't worked out," I tell him vaguely, not sure how much he knows about the current situation.

"I've been talking to some of my colleagues about you," he says. "I got ahold of some tape of you singing that night and they've been very impressed. The label would love for you to come in and talk to them." My eyes widen and my heart starts beating faster.

"Really?" I ask.

"Yes really," he says with a laugh.

"I would love to do that," I gush, realizing how naive I sound.

Clark's eyes light up and I swear that I see dollar signs in them. "I think you could be the next big thing," he says. He sounds so sincere. I want to believe that he has good intentions with this.

"Clark." Jesse says as he walks towards me. Jensen and Tanner follow behind him, their eyes locked on their agent's face. "What are you doing here?" Jesse asks. And the way he asks it comes out more like a threat than anything else.

Clark shifts in his seat uncomfortably. "I was just talking

to Ari about some potential opportunities she has in front of her. The label execs have asked for me to arrange a meeting after seeing her tape of when she performed with you."

"Fuck," Tanner mutters, and my eyes flutter in shock. Why would they think that's a bad thing? Haven't they told me how talented they think I am? How exactly am I supposed to get my start if I never take advantage of any opportunities I have.

"Now's not a good time," says Jesse, and my heart sinks even lower. When I see that Jensen's about to open his mouth, I quickly jump in. "Set up the meeting," I tell Clark, in a tone that I hope leaves no room for argument.

Clark jumps up, obviously wanting to have my answer be the last word in the conversation. "I'll set that up for the band's next break," he says with a crinkle eyed grin. He hustles away before anyone can say anything else.

Jensen grabs my arm and pulls me off the couch towards his dressing room. Tanner and Jesse follow grimly behind.

As soon as the door closes, they start in. "I thought we agreed you would wait. We can set you up with any label you want after this Gentry thing is figured out," says Tanner, pushing an exasperated hand through his hair.

"I want this," I snap, causing all of their eyebrows to raise at my tone. "He's not asking me as a favor to you, he knows you don't want it. He's asking me because he thinks I have talent."

"He's asking you because you're the hottest fucking woman he's ever seen," snaps Jensen.

Tears spring up in my eyes at his comment. He immediately looks like he wishes he could take his comment back, and Jesse and Tanner both look like they're going to kill him. But I don't care. "Is that what you really think? That he couldn't possibly think that I'm talented, it must be related to him doing you a favor or my looks?" I ask.

His mouth moves but nothing comes out. We stare at each

other for what seems like an eternity. "I'm going to wait in the greenroom. Good luck tonight," I whisper in a choked voice as I walk out the door.

To make my night even better, Cassidy is in the greenroom, her lips and hands all over one of the stage crew. *Maybe she can just have Jensen*, I think childishly, before I laugh at my ridiculousness. I will probably jump her if she even lays a hand on Jensen tonight. I'm too close to the edge to deal with groupies on top of everything else.

I nod at one of my security team and leave the room with him following close behind. I'm not going to watch the show tonight. I'm going back to the bus.

In what can only be minutes after the show ended, Jensen comes running onto the bus looking deliciously rumpled from sweating his ass off for hours performing.

"You didn't watch us," he says. "The show sucked."

"I doubt that," I say stiffly.

"It did. Tanner forgot song lyrics the whole time and I played the wrong chord for an entire song without realizing it. Jesse even tripped over one of the chords and fell on stage."

"Seriously?" I ask, figuring he must be joking.

"Seriously," he says, walking over to me and sinking to his knees in front of me in a moment that seems to reverberate from the past. "I'm sorry for being an ass," he says mournfully.

"You basically told me I have no talent," I whisper. "It's like when you laughed at me in high school when I told you my dream of being a singer. I don't think you'll ever believe in me. And maybe that's a sign that I don't have what it takes," I muse, staring off at the wall in front of me.

"Fuck, that's not true. I just...I just was jealous, ok?" he spits out. I look at him confused. "Jealous of Clark? I thought we were past that?" I tell him.

He laughs bitterly. "I wish it was just jealousy of Clark. It's jealousy of everyone. Everyone that is going to see all the pieces that make you who you are. A world is going to fall in love with you. And there's a good chance that you decide that there's something better for you out there. I mean hell, Ari. Who really ends up with their high school sweethearts anymore? I just know that as soon as you're out there, we'll be done. It's one thing to come back to us after you've had an abusive asshole for a husband, it's quite another to stay with us after you see all the options you really have."

He lays his head in my lap after his impassioned speech and I idly stroke his hair as I ponder his words. "There isn't any one on earth that I could love more than the three of you. Don't you get it? It's our past that makes it that way. There's no one else that could ever really know me like you do."

"I don't know everything about you," he says, lifting his head to look me in the eyes. I'm about to respond when Jesse and Tanner storm onto the bus.

Afterwards there's a lot of kissing, a lot of crying on my part, and a lot of forgiveness that occurs. It's all followed by ice cream, more kissing, and late-night movies with the three of them.

I fall asleep in Jensen's lap, relaxed and happy for the first time in a while. In that moment I realize how far we still have to go for our happy ever after. But I can't wait to get there.

ARIANA

I'm standing on the side of the stage, watching the show, when firecrackers startle me. The loud, incessant pop bites into the air over and over again. I look around, confused. We aren't to the part of the show where fireworks go off yet. Some idiot must be outside still tailgating and decided to start the celebration early and is setting them off close to the stadium.

I try to relax back into the music and turn my attention back to the guys. All of a sudden they—bang, bang, BOOM. My whole-body jerks from the enormous explosion. What the hell was that? Swarms of people in the pit start to scream and push, seeking an exit in an unobstructed configuration so they're moving in every direction.

More fireworks—bang, bang, bang—ending with another explosion.

"Ari!" I hear and it's Jensen calling for me. I see the band's personal security team rush out onto the stage to collect the guys. They're fighting against them as they get dragged the opposite direction from where I'm standing.

There's a rush of stage crew and activity around me as

everyone backstage panics as well, and somehow my security team has disappeared. Someone knocks me on the shoulder, causing me to fall to the ground. I hear my name called again but this time I don't look to see where the guys are. Because I see him.

Gentry is standing across the room from me, staring at me with those watery, pale blue eyes I detest so much. He looks satisfied, just like he always did when his fun was about to start, and he had me exactly where he wanted me. I leap to my feet, ready to run away. Screams are echoing in my ears as people continue to panic around us.

But it's like no one else sees him. It's like the two of us are in this alternate world in the midst of everyone else. I freeze when he pulls out a gun. And then I come to my senses and turn to run. Where...I'm not sure. But everything inside of me is telling me to run and hide and wait for the guys to find me. I just couldn't let Gentry get to me.

"Ari," calls Gentry in a sing song voice. Twirling, I look to see where he is, but he's disappeared from where he was standing.

Then, suddenly I see him off to the side of me.

Time slows. I'm living in an alternate reality watching, paralyzed, when Gentry raises his arm and fires two bullets in quick succession into a hapless crew member who happens to cross his path at that moment. I scream as I watch him fall to the ground in an unmoving heap.

But I have little time to process events. Gentry's sure steps are leading directly toward me. Stopping dead in my tracks, a deer in headlights, I'm mesmerized by him. His low baseball cap is pulled around his eyes, but I can see them. They've taken on the red hue of the stage lights still shining behind me. Intent on his target, he plows through the confusion. People rush in every direction, and I'm pushed toward him in their haste to escape. Stopping not ten feet away, a corner of his mouth lifts in a snarl.

"Hello, wife," he says, but I don't hear it. I read the words as his lips move in slow motion. I'm transported back to every time he lifted his hand to hit me, or kicked me, or knocked me out. I remain silent and staring when he lifts his gun. Holding up my hands in weak defense I turn to run and just as I do, two things happen. BOOM! A crack so loud my ears ring and then the force of it hits me. It's a hot pain that's so painful that I can't breathe. My whole chest feels like it's burning. I faintly notice Gentry walking away, no one bothering to stop him in the panic of the moment.

Warm hands suddenly descend upon me and one whispered word has love gripping my heart despite the chill that is starting to descend upon my whole body.

"Ari." The stage lights must go out because the darkness of night descends around us. I feel Jensen come up next to where I'm lying. I move into his body heat, drawing him down in comfort as my breath becomes labored. I'm struck by the sheer terror glazing over his eyes. Dropping his head into the crook of my neck, a small wheeze sharpens the air and heat passes between us. Soft and flowing, a stream runs through, coating my T-shirt and his, gluing us together.

My heart beat slows. My lungs stop aching. Gentry had done it. He had finally killed me. After everything he'd done to me, this was just it...I would be gone.

I was free.

That's when I blacked out.

JENSEN

Each beep punctuates the air with sound, hitting the center of my chest with the knowledge that each beep meant she was still alive. But those beeps were providing more than life for her. Each one enabled me to hold onto my sanity a little bit longer. Her hand was cold and clammy, in mine. Her skin was paler than it would normally be. We had planned on flying her to the Bahamas on our next break. We were going to spend hours by the pool at the resort Jesse had booked to give us a break from the bus. Her skin was going to have that perfect golden glow that only she was capable of.

We weren't going to get the chance to do that now. Her skin was so pale, I could make out the veins that ran from her hands to her elbows, disappearing underneath the hospital gown she wore. I bring her wrist to my mouth and place a kiss on the underside, right on top of the veins that ran from her hand up through her body. After pulling away, I press a thumb to her pulse, taking comfort in feeling its beat against my skin. I drop my head, cradling it in her hand as I breathe deeply. She smells different. That unique Ari smell was missing, replaced by the artificial smells of the hospital. She smells sterile. I hate it. Evidently the lack of smell is the thing that finally makes my chest tighten, makes my throat close up, makes me break. I could have lost her. I still can. A knock sounds on the door behind me.

"Jensen Reid?" The voice was firm, but kind. I lift my head up to look at the doorway. A petite brunette woman walks to the other side of the hospital bed and reaches out her hand to shake mine. "I'm Dr. Rickland. I'm one of the doctors taking care of Ariana."

I nod. I don't want to waste any words, any energy. I'm ready to collapse. Dr. Rickland moves further into the room. She moves smoothly, as if she's walked the same path of tiles over and over, every single day. It's an odd thing to notice, but I guess I'm in an odd place right now.

"I know the ER team already spoke to you earlier, but can you answer a few questions for me? We want to make sure we get a handle on what happened."

What happened? Even I wasn't completely sure. I open my mouth to speak, but the words don't come. I swallow and clear my throat. "Sure." It was all I could manage to say. She nods and takes the seat across from the foot of Ariana's bed. She pulls a notebook from her pocket and smiles gently at me.

"You were the one who got to her first, correct?" I listen to three beeps from the machines before I answer.

"That's correct."

"And you started CPR and put pressure on the wounds, correct?" My mind flashes back to that moment, to when my lips touched hers. Our lips had touched a million times before, but only this time to deliver life, not affection. There had been so much blood.

"Yes."

"Do you know who shot her?" This question had already been asked a half a dozen times. The first time it'd been asked, I had lost it on the police officer who was preventing me from getting to the hospital. I feel a little bad about that. Now that I've calmed down, it was slightly easier to give an answer.

"It was her ex-husband." She nods. "Do you know why he would do that?"

I drop my head, cradling it in my hands. The moment I'd heard the shots and seen her fall had felt like a blur, a dream sequence. Holding her limp body against mine hadn't felt real. It was a moment I couldn't forget.

"They're in the middle of getting a divorce. He was very abusive during their marriage and she had only recently been able to escape. He had been stalking her since she joined the tour with us. We found out last night that our band manager, Miranda Hutchins, had been helping him behind the scenes in the hope that it would scare Ariana and make her leave the tour."

I think back to the moment when Miranda had come into the room where the police where interrogating us about Gentry. There had been mascara running down her cheeks and she had been a far cry from the perfectly put together manager that I had become accustomed to.

"I'm so sorry," she cries as she stands in front of Tanner.

"Can we talk later? We need to finish talking to the police so we can get to the hospital," Tanner snaps at her, trying to gently move her out of the way.

"This is all my fault," she whispers.

"Miranda, what are you even talking about?" Tanner said. "We don't have time for your theatrics right now."

"I've been helping Ariana's ex send her things," she continues, still whispering, her whole-body trembling.

The whole room looks at her in shock. "What?" said Tanner with a growl. The words vomit out of her lips. On and on about how she had fallen in love with Tanner and was just trying to get rid of Ariana so he would notice her. How she hadn't known it would go this far. How Tanner had to forgive her.

It had taken three police officers to get Tanner's hands off Miranda's throat.

"Do you know how long she stopped breathing for?" the doctor asks, bringing my attention back to the present.

That moment is ingrained in my mind, the moment when I felt her chest go still. I should know all the details but I'm pretty sure my brain stopped functioning when that happened.

Before I could tell her as much, she continued. "Was it as long as a commercial break? Or longer?"

I rewound my brain to the moment. I had desperately started pushing on her chest, trying to do anything I could to get her heart to start beating again, to get air in her lungs and to her brain. I remembered before that, to when I had first gotten to her. As I'd neared her, I'd seen the look of utter peace on her face, eyes open, her face relaxed. She'd looked ethereal.

I remembered bits and pieces: the screaming and shouts around me, the ambulance arriving and the paramedics trying to get to Ari, Tanner and Jesse pulling me off because I wouldn't let go of Ari. I remembered frantically checking for a pulse even as the paramedics took her away. I remembered finally being pulled away from her and then watching as she disappeared from sight.

"Jensen." The voice was faint, pulling me out of the memory. I whip my head to the hospital bed, but Ariana's eyes are still closed. My name was said again, and I turn my head to the doctor, likely looking at her with renewed grief.

"It was probably less than a commercial break. Or, I don't know." I rub my hands through my hair in frustration. "Maybe longer? I don't know." The doctor regards me for a moment.

"You saved her life, Jensen." I look at her; pen paused on the paper in her hand. "If she has any chance of making it through with any semblance of the Ariana that she was before it will be because you kept air going through her body."

The doctor's voice was soothing in some way, but it wasn't the voice I wanted to hear the most. I laughed, the sound lacking warmth. "Not without help," I said while gesturing at the ventilator that was wrapped around her face.

"She's in a medically induced coma. We need the swelling in her body to go down to help her systems to heal."

Despite this doctor's words, the last doctor who was in here had already told me that brain damage is likely. They just didn't know the extent. I tell her as much.

"'Likely' is not a word I like to use. It's not very scientific, and I'm a scientist. I go on facts, not assumptions. So have some faith."

"Faith is not very scientific either, Dr. Rickland."

That earns a small smile from her. "No, it's not." She stands up and tucks her notepad into her coat pocket. "But her chest x-rays look surprisingly good for someone who was shot three times, and her blood pressure is stabilizing. The scientist in me feels optimistic at her recovery. You should too."

She walks to the door and stops, spinning elegantly on her rubber soled shoes. "And I want an autograph after she's up and running," she says meaningfully before leaving.

I heave a sigh at the ridiculousness of what she just asked considering the situation, and then bring my attention back to Ariana.

She looks peaceful, with her hands resting on her chest, her red nail polish chipped. Her eyes are closed, her long lashes resting upon the pale skin that looks bruised under her eyes. There were bruises elsewhere on her body from falling to the ground, and I know that under the blanket, her torso was riddled with three bullet wounds. I didn't know what to do with the rage that simmered just under the surface. It bubbled and spilled over, made me think, act, feel irrationally.

The energy rippled through me, over and over, but there was no way to let it out. Gentry was still out there. Even if Ariana lived, he would keep coming after her until the job was done.

Five days pass like this. Jesse is in and out of the room with red-lined eyes, but Tanner stays in the waiting room. I know that I should probably go and talk to him, try to assuage the guilt he was carrying with him thanks to Miranda's actions. Guilt that was even worse because evidently, he had been hiding from Ari and the rest of us how much Miranda had been hitting on him behind the scenes in order to try and protect Ari's feelings.

But I didn't have the energy.

Everything in me was dedicated to the gorgeous girl in the bed next to me. I would leave briefly to shower and grab some coffee, but other than that I stayed in a chair next to her. After all, how could I go far when she was holding my heart hostage, and had been since the day I met her?

Today I had brought a box with me. It was a box that I hadn't shown anyone. It was a box that was meant for her. I pulled off the lid and looked at the stack of letters, two hundred and sixty letters. Letters that I wrote her every week that we were apart leading up to the week before she had appeared at that concert. I had told her a lot of lies in the beginning, like that it was easy to forget her.

The letters were proof that forgetting her had been impossible. I probably would have written her letters for the rest of my life if we had never reunited. She had always been the person that I could tell my secrets to, that I could bare my soul to. Without her, I had been lost. The letters had been a way for me to pretend like she was there listening to me. They were a way for me to get my thoughts out before they overtook me.

I open a few up and read through some of them. The early letters were pained and angry. They were full of heartbroken betrayal and regret. There was one letter where the only words were the lyrics to Hate Me by Blue October. It had been one of our favorite songs and the first time I had heard it on the radio after I lost her, I was a mess for the whole day. I guess that was all I could muster to write that week.

Some of the letters raged at her. They called her all sorts of terrible names that would make her cry if she read them. I flinched when I opened one letter and saw "Bitch" written in large red letters at the top of the page. As time went on, and the pain wasn't as fresh, I could pretend that I was just writing to her while she was away on a trip. The letters talked about what was going on, the songs that I was writing, the stupid things the guys had been up to. They were written like I was just talking to her, and they always ended with how much I missed her.

I got to the last letter that I had written her before she had stormed back into my life. I start to read it out loud even though I know she can't hear me.

M y dearest love,

I t feels good to say that word. There have been very few people that I have loved in my life. But none of them have compared to what I have felt for you. I miss you every day. There's not a moment where I'm not wishing you were here or wondering what you are doing. It's been five years and I don't think I've really lived a day of those years, not really. I've been stuck in the past, hoping that things will change. I'll never tell you this, but I went home a month after you told us goodbye. I had to see you, had to make sure that you were alright. I went by your trailer and your mom answered. I asked where you were, and she went on and on about how you had run off with some guy that you had met and she hadn't seen you since. I didn't believe her but when I went to look in your bedroom, everything you owned was gone.

I went home and burned every picture I had of you.

finish reading the letter with a choked voice, and then I finally look at Ariana. I grab the hand that's not connected to the heart monitor and the iv, and I lay my forehead gently against it, finally letting all the pain of the last few days...of the last few years out as I sob. A series of beeping startles me and I quickly take a look at the heart monitor. The lines are jumping all over the place and I quickly press the call button to let the nurse know something was going on.

All of a sudden, the hand I'm gripping moves, and it almost feels like she had squeezed my hand. I look out the door anxiously, hoping that a nurse would come by soon.

"Jensen."

My heart stops in the moment it took for me to look from the door to the bed. Ariana's golden eyes stare back at me.

"Hi," she whispers.

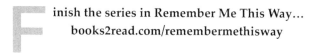

inish the series in Remember Me This Way…
books2read.com/remembermethisway

REMEMBER ME
THIS WAY

Conclude Ariana's journey with the Sound of Us in Remember Me This Way...out now! Books2read.com/remembermethisway

AUTHOR'S NOTE

Book 2 is done! This book has been the hardest that I've written so far because of some health issues. But I made it through! There's a lot to cover in Book 3, but I'm so excited about the journey these characters are taking with us. Book 3 is Tanner's book, but it's also about Ari's growth. She's come so far since the beginning and I can't wait for you to see how she ends up.

I once read that authors have a theme that they use in every story. I think mine would be the question of whether the past is ever really as good as you remember. For Ari and her guys, the question is whether a high school love can translate into an adult life able to withstand the pressures of the everyday.

I think that Ari and her guys can.

I'd like to thank my Beta Team: Nichol, Caitlin, Jess, and Tiffany. They are always willing to let me bounce ideas off of them and they tell me when my teasers are too long (haha).

I'd also like to thank my Arc Team. You guys are the bomb. Your reviews literally make me tear up and I'm so thankful you are all willing to jump in and suggest my books and promo me. You are the best!

P.S. Read on after this page to get the first chapters of my completed enemies to lovers duet, Heartbreak Prince!

SNEAK PREVIEW OF HEARTBREAK PRINCE

Keep reading for a sneak preview of Heartbreak Prince, my complete enemies to lovers duet.

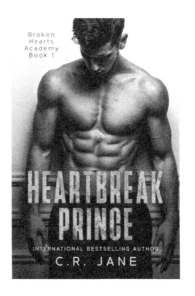

Heartbreak Prince by C. R. Jane

Copyright © 2020 by C. R. Jane

All rights reserved.

No portion of this book may be reproduced in any form or by any electronic or mechanical means, including information storage and retrieval systems, without written permission from the author, except for the use of brief quotations in a book review, and except as permitted by U.S. copyright law.

For permissions contact:

crjaneauthor@gmail.com

This book is a work of fiction. Names, characters, businesses, places, events, locales, and incidents are either the products of the author's imagination or used in a fictitious manner. Any resemblance to actual persons, living or dead, or actual events is purely coincidental.

HEARTBREAK PRINCE

Soulmates. I believe in them. I was lucky enough to have two of them at one point.

The only problem. *My soulmates happened to be twin brothers.*

Caiden was the light to Jackson's dark. And after all that I had been through, the light was what I thought I needed.

When I chose Caiden, I lost Jackson.

Feeling like half a person after Jackson left, I barely survived when tragedy struck and I lost Caiden too.

It took me years to admit to myself that I had chosen wrong from the beginning. I'm ready to admit it to Jackson… only problem, he hates me.

I'm ready to fight for my happily ever after.

But there's a reason they call him the Heartbreak Prince.

I lost my virginity to an angel...but my first and last kiss was with the devil.
And that's everything you need to know about me.

Sometimes when it's really dark outside, and I feel particularly alone. I allow myself to remember us. It doesn't happen often, because I wouldn't be able to function otherwise, but I just wanted you to know that everything about us is like perfect Technicolor in my memory.

CHAPTER 1

THEN

was eight when we met. *Do you remember that?* I was in third grade. I was small for my age, and all the other kids picked on me. They had plenty of things to go after— who my father was, my slight lisp, how my clothes were all too baggy, and how I didn't have a running washing machine at my house, and so oftentimes my clothes weren't quite as clean as they should have been...because washing clothes in the sink could only go so far. All were fair game. My class-mates had made my life a living hell all through elementary school. And I expected it to continue...until the two of you started school.

You started a new school that year. You and your brother had just moved into town. You were only a few months older than me, but you weren't scared of anything. And when you saw me on the playground, and you saw how some of the kids had picked up rocks from the ground and were going to throw them at me, you marched right in. And while Caiden was yelling at them to stop, you were the one who actually tackled Marshall, the biggest kid, who had been particularly awful to me for years. And you didn't even know me.

And when you got up after punching him several times,

your lip was bleeding, but you gave me the biggest smile and told me it was all going to be okay.

Do you remember that?

Neither of us noticed the fact that Caiden was also looking at me.

Wasn't it funny how a story like ours could happen like that, even at that young of an age?

We were best friends after you and Caiden defended me that day. Maybe the two of you were more than best friends to me, maybe you were my saviors. Because after years of living in hell, you made sure that school became my safe place.

Remember how Caiden always used to bring extra for lunch, and pretend that he wasn't hungry, but he would actually give it to me? I was in the free lunch program, but both of you thought the school lunches were disgusting and wouldn't allow me to eat them. You never noticed how I snuck the cafeteria food in my backpack after I ate what Caiden brought because if I didn't, I wouldn't have had dinner.

Do you remember how you would beg your parents to let me come over? And even though I was dirty and small, and your parents wished you had other friends, you told them that I was yours, and somehow, you got them to listen.

What you didn't know, or you refused to see, was that Caiden also begged your parents just as fiercely, and he also told them that I was his.

I just wanted you to know that if I had known how it all would've ended up, even at eight years old, I would've run as far away from the two of you as I could.

After I turned ten, Dorothy Miller announced to the whole school at lunch that she was going to marry you. So I punched her.

Do you remember that?

For some reason, the cool thing that fall was for everyone to pretend to get married. But you and Caiden were who all the popular girls wanted to marry.

You got jealous because Caiden asked me to marry him first, so you went ahead and pretended to marry Dorothy, even though it made me cry.

Remember showing up at the pretend ceremony during recess? How Caiden stood there looking so serious—well, as serious as an eleven-year-old boy could—and he promised me he was going to love me forever and ever.

You laughed along with the other kids, who laughed because they all knew it was a joke that someone like Caiden would ever really love someone like me.

Remember when you found me crying afterwards, because it was the first time you'd ever laughed at me? Then you started crying because you felt so bad. You told me that even if Caiden loved me, you were going to love me forever and ever, too.

Then you told me you just wanted me to know that you would love me more, no matter what.

And even at ten, I wanted you to kiss me.

When I was twelve, things grew even worse at home. I didn't tell you, because the whole thing was really embarrassing. But you saw bruises on me, and I knew you didn't believe me when I told you I fell down at recess every day playing soccer.

You started walking me home every day after that first time I lied to you. That first day, your parents didn't know where you went, because you hadn't told Caiden, or asked permission. They found us halfway to my house. Your mom was shrieking, because she was so scared. You looked right at her and told her that you had to protect me.

Remember how Caiden got out of the car and hugged me because I was upset that you'd gotten in trouble? Remember how Caiden begged your mom to give me a ride home every day? Remember how she said that she couldn't because she didn't know my mom?

That year was really hard. Maybe all the other years were hard too. But I think what stuck out in my mind about that year was that it was the first time I realized how big the difference between us really was. I had never seen your mom's Range Rover before. I think Mama had sold her car by then to help pay the property taxes on our home.

I told myself in that moment that no matter what, I would keep a small part of myself away from the two of you.

Then you pitched a big fit, and your mom agreed to drop me off that one time, and I realized how hard keeping myself separate from you was going to be.

I was thirteen when Caiden told me you kissed Marcy Thomas. I confronted you and told you that you had ruined everything. I screamed at you about doing it, and you tried to tell me that Marcy was the one that had kissed you. But I didn't care.

We were supposed to be each other's first kiss.

And so when Caiden kissed me under the bleachers a week later...I kissed him back.

It was a fumbling kiss, but still a really good one. And Caiden told me he loved me again, and this time it wasn't because of a fake marriage ceremony. I told him I loved him back, because I did.

But even then, I knew it probably wasn't the same kind of love that he was talking about.

When I got home that night, you don't know this, but I cried. I cried because I wished the whole time that I had been kissing you.

CHAPTER 2

NOW

Beeeeeep. Beeeeeep.

The sound of the hospital equipment ground on my nerves more than usual. Why did I do this to myself? Why did I come every week to sit by the bedside of my former boyfriend? Guilt?

After all, it was my fault he ended up here. It was my fault that the world would never see his wide smile, or the dimple that was only on one cheek.

I thought the guilt would fade in time, release itself the way that sorrow and loss often do. But that hadn't been the case. It had been two years, five months, and eighteen days since I last saw his smile. And even then, the aftermath of what happened that night remained emblazoned in my mind, just as vivid as if it happened yesterday.

The memory of his smile had faded though. All I could remember now was the stark grief on his face now when we last spoke.

He should have been taken off the machine years ago, but his parents hadn't been able to do it. One thing was for certain, you couldn't accuse Caiden's parents of neglect. This room was proof of that, more like a shrine than a hospital bed at this point.

I usually came on Fridays, a punishment of sorts, so I would make sure not to be too happy over the weekend. Which really was stupid, because being "too happy" had never been a threat in my life. I was here on a Monday morning, though, today. It marked a special occasion.

Because in just an hour, I would be starting at a new school, and in just an hour, I would see *him*.

Caiden had always known how to handle Jackson. That brand of darkness inside Jackson, unfathomable to so many, had never frightened Caiden. In a way, they were foils of each other. Fraternal twins and the exact opposites. It always caught people off guard though at how sunny Caiden's disposition had always been. With his black as night hair and even darker brown eyes, he stood in sharp contrast to Jackson's sun god looks.

Maybe his Apollo-like aspect was what threw everyone off about Jackson. Going by his looks alone, he should have been happiness and light personified. So when he went black and savagely punched you in the head and knocked you out because you looked at him wrong...you didn't see it coming.

I fiddled with the blanket on Caiden's bed.

"I think I have to stop coming here," I said softly to his prone form.

For a moment, I almost expected him to answer me.

Of course he didn't. He wouldn't answer me ever again.

At least, that was what the doctors thought. His parents still held out hope for a miracle.

"I think it's time for me to move on," I continued. And it was a relief that he couldn't answer back.

Because what people didn't know about Caiden was that underneath his wide smile was a boy who couldn't let me go.

He called me the loveliest kind of pain.

I called him a monster.

Continue the story at books2read.com/heartbreakprince

JOIN C.R.'S FATED REALM

Visit my **Facebook** page to get updates.

Visit my **Amazon Author** page.

Visit my website at www.crjanebooks.com

Sign up for my **newsletter** to stay updated on new releases, find out random facts about me, and get access to different points of view from my characters.

BOOKS BY C.R. JANE

www.crjanebooks.com

The Sounds of Us Contemporary Series (complete series)

Remember Us This Way

Remember You This Way

Remember Me This Way

Broken Hearts Academy Series: A Bully Romance (complete duet)

Heartbreak Prince

Heartbreak Lover

Ruining Dahlia (Contemporary Mafia Standalone)

Ruining Dahlia

The Fated Wings Series (Paranormal series)

First Impressions

Forgotten Specters

The Fallen One (a Fated Wings Novella)

Forbidden Queens

Frightful Beginnings (a Fated Wings Short Story)

Faded Realms

Faithless Dreams

Fabled Kingdoms

Fated Wings 8

The Rock God (a Fated Wings Novella)

The Darkest Curse Series

Forget Me

Lost Passions

Hades Redemption Series

The Darkest Lover

The Darkest Kingdom

Monster & Me Duet Co-write with Mila Young

Monster's Temptation

Monster's Obsession

Academy of Souls Co-write with Mila Young (complete series)

School of Broken Souls

School of Broken Hearts

School of Broken Dreams

School of Broken Wings

Fallen World Series Co-write with Mila Young (complete series)

Bound

Broken

Betrayed

Belong

Thief of Hearts Co-write with Mila Young (complete series)

Darkest Destiny

Stolen Destiny

Broken Destiny

Sweet Destiny

Kingdom of Wolves Co-write with Mila Young

Wild Moon

Wild Heart

Wild Girl

Wild Love

Wild Soul

Stupid Boys Series Co-write with Rebecca Royce

Stupid Boys

Dumb Girl

Crazy Love

Breathe Me Duet Co-write with Ivy Fox (complete)

Breathe Me

Breathe You

Rich Demons of Darkwood Series Co-write with May Dawson

Make Me Lie

Make Me Beg

Make Me Wild

Printed in Great Britain
by Amazon